A Book Of

CASES IN HUMAN RESOURCE MANAGEMENT

For BBA : Semester VI
As Per New Syllabus w.e.f. 2015

Mr. Suresh Muke
B.Com., DBM, MBA

NIRALI PRAKASHAN
ADVANCEMENT OF KNOWLEDGE

N3471

Cases in Human Resource Management (BBA - VI)   ISBN 978-93-5164-845-1

First Edition : **January 2016**

© : **Author**

Published By :   Polyplet

NIRALI PRAKASHAN

Abhyudaya Pragati, 1312, Shivaji Nagar,
Off J.M. Road, PUNE – 411005
Tel - (020) 25512336/37/39, Fax - (020) 25511379
Email : niralipune@pragationline.com

☞ DISTRIBUTION CENTRES

PUNE

Nirali Prakashan : 119, Budhwar Peth, Jogeshwari Mandir Lane, Pune 411002, Maharashtra
Tel : (020) 2445 2044, 66022708, Fax : (020) 2445 1538
Email : bookorder@pragationline.com, niralilocal@pragationline.com

Nirali Prakashan : S. No. 28/27, Dhyari, Near Pari Company, Pune 411041
Tel : (020) 24690204 Fax : (020) 24690316
Email : dhyari@pragationline.com, bookorder@pragationline.com

MUMBAI

Nirali Prakashan : 385, S.V.P. Road, Rasdhara Co-op. Hsg. Society Ltd.,
Girgaum, Mumbai 400004, Maharashtra
Tel : (022) 2385 6339 / 2386 9976, Fax : (022) 2386 9976
Email : niralimumbai@pragationline.com

☞ DISTRIBUTION BRANCHES

JALGAON

Nirali Prakashan : 34, V. V. Golani Market, Navi Peth, Jalgaon 425001,
Maharashtra, Tel : (0257) 222 0395, Mob : 94234 91860

KOLHAPUR

Nirali Prakashan : New Mahadvar Road, Kedar Plaza, 1st Floor Opp. IDBI Bank
Kolhapur 416 012, Maharashtra. Mob : 9850046155

NAGPUR

Pratibha Book Distributors : Above Maratha Mandir, Shop No. 3, First Floor,
Rani Jhanshi Square, Sitabuldi, Nagpur 440012, Maharashtra
Tel : (0712) 254 7129

DELHI

Nirali Prakashan : 4593/21, Basement, Aggarwal Lane 15, Ansari Road, Daryaganj
Near Times of India Building, New Delhi 110002
Mob : 08505972553

BENGALURU

Pragati Book House : House No. 1, Sanjeevappa Lane, Avenue Road Cross,
Opp. Rice Church, Bengaluru – 560002.
Tel : (080) 64513344, 64513355,Mob : 9880582331, 9845021552
Email:bharatsavla@yahoo.com

CHENNAI

Pragati Books : 9/1, Montieth Road, Behind Taas Mahal, Egmore,
Chennai 600008 Tamil Nadu, Tel : (044) 6518 3535,
Mob : 94440 01782 / 98450 21552 / 98805 82331,
Email : bharatsavla@yahoo.com

niralipune@pragationline.com | www.pragationline.com

Also find us on 🆕 www.facebook.com/niralibooks

Preface ...

Human Resource management is a significant concept which states that people are the fundamental force behind a well-organised industry. Case studies in Human Resource Management provide information on different situations and issues regarding various subjects that are related to Human resource. Case Studies help students to understand the issues related to people and give proper solutions to run an organisation successfully or perform better.

The present book has been designed with a goal to provide meaningful insight into the case studies in Human Resource Management relating to topics like Recruitment and Selection Wage Administration, Performance management, Grievance handling and Labour Welfare.

It gives me a feeling of immense pleasure and gratitude when placing before the students of BBA and other readers, the book of Cases in Human Resource Management. It is based on the revised syllabus for BBA.

I would like to express my sincere thanks to Mr. Jignesh Furia and the entire staff of Nirali Prakashan for the encouragement and help in bringing out this book.

We are sure that the book will be a good guidance to the students. We will be thankful and will welcome any suggestions for the improvement in any of the contents of the book. We are quite confident that this text book will receive the patronage of all for whom it is intended.

Authors

Syllabus ...

Unit 1: Introduction to Case Studies:

Case – Meaning – Objectives of Case Studies – Characteristics and Importance of Case Studies – Cases Discussion.

Guidelines for Analyzing Case Studies on the following points

- Facts of the case
- Analysis
- Solution
- Action points
- Conclusion

Unit 2: Topics for Case studies:-

1. Recruitment and Selection
2. Training and Development
3. Working conditions
4. Salary and Wage Administration - Pay scales and Grades
5. Performance Management System
6. Grievance Handling
7. Settlement of Industrial disputes-Industrial Relations
8. Transfer - Promotion - Demotion
9. Labor Welfare
10. Retrenchment - Layoffs
11. VRS

***

Contents ...

***

Chapter **1** ...

Introduction to Case Studies

Contents ...

Learning Objectives

- To understand the meaning of Case Studies
- To analyse and understand the objectives of a Case Study
- To learn about the characteristics of a Case Study
- To study in detail about the various types of Case Studies
- To know more about the limitations of a Case Study
- To understand the guidelines to solve a Case Study

1.1 Introduction to Case Studies

1.1.1 Introduction

Cast study is usually a method, a move towards social reality and a technique of organising data with regard to some chosen units. According to **Pauline V. Young**, a thorough study of an individual or group is called a life or case history. In this sense, a complete study of a social unit like an individual, a group, a social institution, a district or a community is known as a case study.

Thus, each circumstance, whether it is a complete life cycle or a specific process of this cycle, forms part of a case study and the dependent factors as situations. The technique by which we collect information concerning 'total' situation or combination of interrelated factors by which we explain the social processes or sequences of events or by which we try the individual behaviour in its social surroundings and analyse and compare cases leading to generalisations or formation of principles, is called as a case study method.

It is important to mention the views of **William J. Goode and Paul K. Hatt**. They believed that case study is a way of organising social data in order to protect the unitary character of the social object that is being studied. Spoken somewhat differently, it is an approach which sees any social unit as a whole. This approach consists of the development of a unit, which may be an individual or a family or other social group, a sect of relationships or processes or even a complete culture. Case study is, thus, a method which considers all relevant aspects of a situation employed as the unit of study. It tries to understand the interaction of different difficult variables and considers the addition of a similar logic to the total phenomena.

1.1.2 Meaning of Case Studies

A case is generally a "description of a real situation, commonly involving a decision, a challenge, an opportunity, a problem or an issue faced by a person or individuals in an organisation." It is also an effective way to sensitise the students and faculty to the difficulties and structures of commercial business organisations and leadership conditions. Business cases are one of the most effectual and suitable ways to introduce practice into the classroom, to tap an extensive range of experiences, and to dynamically engage students in analysis and decision-making. The cases are not meant to be as examples of either weak or very good management practices. Nor do they give examples of specific concepts.

By design, case studies generally take as their main subject selected examples of a social entity within its normal context. At the easiest level, the case study gives descriptive accounts of one or more cases yet can also be used in a rational way to attain experimental isolation of one or more selected social factors within a real-life context.

1.1.3 Definitions of Case Study

Case study is a way of organising social data so as to preserve the unitary character of the social object being studied. Expressed somewhat differently it is an approach which views any social unit as a whole. **– William J. Goode and Paul K. Hatt**

Case study method may be defined as a small inclusive and intensive study of an individual in which investigator brings to bear all his skills and methods or as a systematic gathering of enough information about a person to permit one to understand how he or she functions as a unit of society. **– Hsin Pao Yang**

The case study is a form of qualitative analysis involving the very careful and complete observation of a person, a situation or an institution. **– John Biesanz and Mavis Biesanz**

1.1.4 Objectives of Case Study

The objectives of the case method are to:

1. **Help acquire skills** of putting the information of management that is gained from the textbook into practice. The managers do not achieve much because of what they know but because of what they do.

2. **Diagnose problems and evaluate alternatives** to get you out of the habit of being a recipient of facts, ideas and methods and get into the habit of diagnosing problems, analysing and evaluating alternatives, and making effective plans of action.

3. **Train** you to work out answers and solutions for yourselves, as opposed to depending upon the reliable crutch of the teacher/counsellor or a textbook.

4. **Provide you exposure** to various organisations and managerial circumstances (which might take a lifetime to experience personally), hence providing you a foundation for comparison in your working as a career manager.

1.1.5 Characteristics of a Case Study

1. **Tell a story:** Case studies stories are told to prove something or teach a lesson. They describe a journey. One that has a clear start and end. In this journey, the audience learns about various heroes, villains, barriers, extraordinary actions and imaginative thinking. At the end, a significant change results.

2. **Have a logic flow:** Instead of chapters, case studies follow a design that sets up a logic flow. The right design is one that teaches the lesson you want the

audience to study. It can be as easy as a situation, solution, results or customer, challenge, journey, discovery, solution, implementation, results or one that is more customised to your required result.

3. **Resolve problem:** The logic flow clarifies a problem that is resolved. At the start, great case studies give an outlook and context that completely describe the problem. Who is the company? What do they do? What is the problem they were encountering? How is this circumstance different from the past? Why is this important to your business? This establishes reliability and relevance with the audience and makes the resolution have more effect at the end.

4. **Focus on the customer:** The customer is always the problem and the resolution at the core, particularly their association with the firm or brand. In most cases, the firm's connection with the customer has changed. Maybe the firm stopped paying attention or customer requirements changed or they have outgrown the product or service the firm offers. But there is something that has been lost that has to be found in an innovative way.

5. **Present inspiring actions:** One of the most significant parts of case studies is the action the firm takes to rise above their problem. It must be reasonable but philosophical; smart, imaginative and must inspire the audience to do something similar for their firm.

6. **Avoid jargon:** Case studies avoid terms such as "market leading" and "unique." No one believes them. They reduce reliability and relevance.

7. **Are grounded in hard facts:** The conclusion for all case studies is results. They consist of statistics to explain the difference made and benefits achieved. The hard facts show how the actions that are implemented generate real-life results. Ballpark figures and/or indexes are fine.

8. **Are capable of being skimmed:** More than one case study is usually given to pinpoint something and teach a lesson. You may be presenting them or your viewers may read them without you. Organise and write case studies so it's simple for your viewers to get the facts you want them to take away.

9. **Work as sales tools:** Case studies are not about admiring past work as much as encouraging new views. Whether you are accountable for the case study or just telling the story, case studies are a reflection of the kind of challenge you respond to, thinking you admire and the results you identify as significant.

10. **Have a call-to-action:** The lessons in case studies are intended to motivate others to action. It's best to help them in taking the first step with a call-to-action with what you or your firm offers.

1.1.6 Types of Case Studies

1. **Explanatory:** This type of case study would be used if you were trying to answer a question that sought to explain the supposed causal connections in real-life interventions that are too difficult for the survey or experimental strategies. In the language of an evaluation, the descriptions would connect program implementation with program effects.

2. **Exploratory:** This type of case study is used to look at those circumstances in which the intervention being assessed has no clear, single set of results.

3. **Multiple case studies:** A multiple case study allows the researcher to look at the differences within and between cases. The objective is to make a copy of the findings across cases. Because comparisons will be drawn, it is important that the cases are selected carefully so that the researcher can forecast similar outcomes across cases, or foresee contrasting outcomes based on a theory.

4. **Representative cases:** The first and most common form of case study is the representative case – the study of a distinctive, standard example of a wider group. This is the workhorse of case study designs, as helpful as it is undramatic.

5. **Prototypical cases:** The second type of case study is the prototypical form. Here a subject is selected not because it is representative but because it is expected to become so: "their present is our future". Studying an early example may help us in knowing about a phenomenon of growing importance.

6. **Deviant cases:** Deviant case studies are based on different reasons from both representative and prototypical designs. The reason for a deviant case study is to throw light on the extraordinary and the untypical: the countries which remain communist, or which are still ruled by the military, or which appear to be protected from democratising fashions.

7. **Instrumental cases:** These are used to achieve something other than understanding a specific condition. It provides insight into a problem or helps in refining a theory. The case is of minor interest; it plays a supportive role, promoting our understanding of something else. The case is frequently explored thoroughly, its contexts examined, its ordinary activities detailed, and because it helps the researcher in pursuing the external interest. The case may or may not be seen as typical of other cases.

8.   **Single case study:** When a single case is studied in depth, it is called as a single case study. A single case study may be exploratory, descriptive or explanatory. At times it is used to check a theory.

9.   **Comparative or Multiple case studies:** Instead of a single case, if the researcher learns two or more than two cases in depth it may be known as a comparative case study or multiple case studies. Multiple case studies allow a researcher to check a single theory more than once. Thus, it has more explanatory control than a single case study. For some cases, similar results will be forecasted; for others, different results.

     Normal, abnormal, positive and negative studies are other types.

10. **Informational type case studies:** These consist of various items like working environment, inter-organisational context, co-ordination activities, problem areas, history of events, inhibiting factors on decision-making, etc. This type boosts the awareness about the environment, assists in the decision-making process. This also helps in assessing the results of the decision.

11. **Appraisal cases:** This type involves problem-solving and decision-making.

12. **Project cases:** These are cases with radical educational process involving communication.

13. **Live and Experimental cases or Functional cases:** These types of cases involve social welfare, rehabilitation or introduction of ideas and analytical concepts. These types of cases assist in analysing socio/psychic problems like drug addiction, alcoholism, etc.

     Whatever be the type of case study, just as a doctor detects the disease by a significant examination and does not go about merely by symptoms, one should go about locating the actual problem by a detailed study of the case rather than a surface study of the symptoms and then search for solutions. There will be some specific areas of agreement and some of disagreement. Once we list these symptoms, we would be capable of detecting the actual problem and the solutions therefore.

14. **Diverse case study:** The diverse case study is different to the usual case study for the generation of cross-case hypotheses. On a general level, the ideal diverse case study engages two cases that span the complete array of scores on the cause and/or the result, depending on the research goa and the level of analysis.

1.1.7 Importance of Case Study

Several courses use case studies in their syllabus to teach content, engage students with real life information or give opportunities for students to put themselves in the decision maker's shoes. The merits of a case study are as follows:

1. **Real world context:** Not only do students see how the course material is implemented in the world outside the classroom, they also get to see how the information is frequently vague or not clearly defined in many circumstances.

2. **Explore multiple perspectives:** Cases in which a decision is necessary can be used to expose students to different perspectives from multiple sources and see why people may desire different results. The students can also see how a decision will affect different members, both positively and negatively.

3. **Requires critical thinking and analysis:** Cases generally need students to analyse the data so as to reach a conclusion. Since many assignments are open-ended, students can practice selecting suitable analytic methods as well.

4. **Students synthesise content:** Several cases require students to pull in different analytic techniques and information from different areas of the course so as to give an effective solution to the problem. In addition, a case assignment can require an initial statement of the information and methods used to reach the conclusion.

5. **Intensive in nature:** Case study technique is intensive in nature. It takes up the study of a unit in its entirety. As such, it leaves greater scope for an in depth study of a specific problem.

6. **Aids to study complex problems:** Case studies are important when one is looking for help on a problem in which inter-relationships of numerous factors are involved, and in which it is difficult to know about the individual factors without considering their connections with each other. For example, suppose the rate of capacity utilisation of cement factories in Andhra Pradesh is decreasing, it is better to study a few units to understand as to why it is occurring.

7. **Comprehensive study:** Inferences are confined from the study of a complete situation; an entity, rather than from the study of one or many selected aspects alone. In case of people, it handles different aspects of one's life from the past to the present of an individual systematically.

8. **Describes a real event:** A case study is a report of an actual event or situation, unlike other studies which may engage abstraction from real circumstances.

9. **Helps find deviations:** The case study technique helps in finding out the deviant units which are marginal and are not compared with the amount of data given by the general cases.

10. **More accurate:** This technique is more accurate, as it gets the right information by approaching the unit or units that are under study. Probably as a result of the longer, more personal friendship of the researcher and respondent, it is possible to go deeper into the issues.

11. **Aids sampling:** The case method is helpful in sampling, because it categorises the units well on the basis of their qualifications or features.

12. **Aids questionnaire preparation**: It helps in making the questionnaire more problem-oriented. In-depth study of cases allows the researcher to get adequate understanding of the problem that leads to the formation of a precise schedule or questionnaire for similar studies.

Case study assists in forming a valid hypothesis. When different cases are carefully studied and analysed, the researcher can reach different generalisations, which may be developed into useful hypothesis. In truth, study of the relevant literature and case study are the only two potent sources of hypotheses.

Case study is useful in framing the questionnaire, schedule or other forms. If a questionnaire is drafted after a detailed case study, we can know the oddities of the group plus the individual units, the type of response expected to be available, and ikes and dislikes of the people.

Case study is useful in stratification of the sample. By studying the individual units in detail, we can put them in the exact classes or types.

1.1.8 Limitations of Case Study

Case method has often been criticised on the basis of following limitations.

1. **The first and the primary complexity:** The one that is the basis of all other, is the overconfidence that the researcher forms in his mind. In case of statistical studies, the researcher knows his limitations. He understands that he has learnt only one part of the problem, and there may be others too. Thus, he is adequately careful and alert. In a case study, he learns each unit in its complete dimension. The researcher thus, begins to feel as if he understands everything about the unit and requires no more explanation about it. It is quite comparable to our feeling of belief about our neighbours or close friends whom we have stayed with for years together. Obviously, we start feeling that we understand everything about them, but in reality the most important part of their life is concealed from us. Even two brothers who have lived together for long years do not know about the experiences and influences that have shaped

their life. It is thus clear that a case study, with all its faults and limitations, develops a false sense of confidence which is extremely harmful to any scientific viewpoint.

2. **Generalisations:** These are drawn from a very small number of cases. Thus, what the researcher considers to be the common characteristic of human nature may be personal irregularity of the subject and so, valid for a specific person under particular situations.

3. **The method is quite loose and unsystematic:** No controls are used upon the informant or the researcher. The information that is gathered in this way is usually incompetent of verification and the generalisations drawn from it are also not very precise.

4. **Inaccurate observation:** There is sufficient scope for mistakes because of inaccurate observation and faulty deduction, selection of a case that is not distinctive to the group, mistakes in reporting, failures of the memory, unconscious oversight or repression of unlikeable facts, an inclination to dramatise information, and describe what is more imaginary than real. Under such conditions the information gathered and the deductions drawn are sometimes far from being valid.

5. **Ad hoc theorising:** The researcher develops an inclination towards *ad hoc* theorising. Instead of finding some scientific justification to a specific phenomenon he tries to find some explanation that is reasonable. He is so overconfident because of his intimate knowledge of the unit, that he starts presuming that even his common sense or instinctive descriptions, are most scientific. Such descriptions are unable to verify and are barely reliable.

6. **The time and money needed for case study is much greater than in other methods:** Even if 100 cases are studied under this technique, it would almost take two years. It may not only involve big financial expenditure, but there is also the issue of cases getting astray.

7. **Too lengthy:** Although rich, thick explanation and analysis of a phenomenon may be required, a researcher may not have the time or money to take such a responsibility. And assuming time is available to generate an important case study, the product may be too long, too detailed, or too involved for busy policy makers and practitioners to read and use. The amount of explanation, analysis, or summary material required is up to the investigator. The researcher also must decide about:

    (a) How much of the report is to be made a story?

    (b) How much to compare with other cases?

    (c) How much should one formalise generalisations or leave such generalising to readers?

    (d) How much of the explanation of the researcher should be included in the report? And

    (e) Whether or not and how much to protect anonymity?"

8. **Data not generalised to the population:** One of the main criticisms is that the information that is gathered cannot necessarily be generalised to the larger population. This leads to information being gathered over longitudinal case studies not always being relevant or specifically helpful.

9. **Bias in data collection:** Case studies are usually on one individual, but there also tends to only be one experimenter that gathers the information. This can lead to bias in data collection, which can influence results more in different designs.

1.1.9 Guidelines to Solve a Case Study

1. **Read the case thoroughly:** To completely know about what is happening in a case, it is important to read the case carefully and in detail. You may want to read the case quite fast the first time to get an overview of the industry, the firm, the people, and the circumstances. Read the case again more slowly, making notes as you go.

2. **Define the central issue:** Several cases will have many issues or problems. Recognise the significant problems and divide them from the more insignificant issues. After recognising a major underlying issue, inspect the related problems in the functional areas (for example, marketing, finance, personnel, and so on). Functional area problems may assist you in recognising deep-rooted problems that are the responsibility of the top management.

3. **Define the firm's goals:** Inconsistencies between a firm's goals and its performance may further emphasise the problems that were discovered in step 2. At the very least, recognising the company's goals will provide a guide for the remaining analysis.

4. **Identify the constraints to the problem:** The constraints may limit the solutions that are available to the company. Typical constraints consist of restricted finances, lack of extra production capacity, employee limitations,

strong competitors, relationships with suppliers and customers, and so on. Constraints have to be taken into account when recommending a solution.

5. **Identify all the relevant alternatives:** The list should have all the relevant options that could solve the problem(s) that were recognised in step 2. Use your creativity in finding alternative solutions. Even when solutions are recommended in the case, you may be capable of suggesting better solutions.

6. **Select the best alternative:** Assess each alternative while considering the available information. If you have carefully taken the ensuing five steps, a good solution to the case should be clear. Stand firm against the temptation to jump to this step early in the case analysis. You will possibly miss significant details, misunderstand the problem, or leave out what may be the best alternative solution. You will also need to explain the logic you used to select one alternative and decline the others.

7. **Develop an implementation plan:** The final step in the analysis is to develop a plan for effectively implementing your decision. Lack of an implementation plan even for a very good decision can cause a problem for a company and for you. Don't ignore this step. Your teacher will certainly ask you or someone in the class to explain how to implement the decision.

Points to Remember

*   **A case** is generally a "description of a real situation, commonly involving a decision, a challenge, an opportunity, a problem or an issue faced by a person or individuals in an organisation."

*   The **case study** is a form of qualitative analysis involving the very careful and complete observation of a person, a situation or an institution.

*   **Characteristics of a Case Study**
    1. Tell a story.
    2. Have a logic flow.
    3. Resolve problems.
    4. Completely focus on the customer.
    5. Present inspiring actions.
    6. Avoid jargon.
    7. Are capable of being skimmed.
    8. Work as sales tools.

- **Explanatory case study** would be used if you were trying to answer a question that is too difficult for the survey or experimental strategies.

- **Exploratory case study** is used to look at those circumstances in which the intervention being assessed has no clear, single set of results.

- **Multiple-case study** allows the researcher to look at the differences within and between cases.

- **Representative cases** are the study of a distinctive, standard example of a wider group.

- **Deviant cases** are based on different reasons from both representative and prototypical designs. The reason for a deviant case study is to throw light on the extraordinary and the untypical.

- **Instrumental cases** are used to achieve something other than understanding a specific condition.

- **Single case study** is when a single case is studied in depth.

- **Live and Experimental cases or Functional cases** involve social welfare, rehabilitation or introduction of ideas and analytical concepts.

- **Diverse case study** engages two cases that span the complete array of scores on the cause and/or the result, depending on the research goal and the level of analysis.

- **Project cases** are the cases with radical educational process involving communication.

Questions for Discussion

1. What are the various objectives of a case study?
2. Analyse the importance of a case study.
3. Explain in detail the various types of case studies.
4. Describe the various limitations of a case study.
5. What are the various guidelines to solve a case study?

$\mathcal{C}hapter$ **2**...

Case Studies

Contents ...

2.1 Recruitment and Selection

Case 1: A Case on Recruitment Policy

Delite Crafts Limited is a medium-sized company which was into manufacturing decorative fittings used for homes and offices. It had 500 workers and 45 officers on roll. The company had a well-defined policy for recruitment. Most of the employees joined Delite Crafts Limited as trainees for one year. After evaluating their performance every month and after the successful completion of training, they were absorbed at entry level in the organisation.

In the case of workmen, they were selected as trainee operators and in the case of officers, they were designated either as trainee officers or manager trainees. Usually, the higher level posts were filled through promotions or sometimes with transfers from other companies owned by the group. As per the practice, direct recruitment was avoided, specifically, at the managerial level. If a suitable candidate was not found within the company, then and only then, an advertisement was given in the newspapers and thereafter, after fulfilling the basic formalities, the person appropriate for the post was selected.

As the real estate business was growing very rapidly, the company with a view to capitalising on the same, was busy making product expansion plans. They were considering new designs, patterns and styles, particularly, for the bathroom, doors and other general fittings for expansion of business. Therefore, the said company decided to recruit two design engineers for business expansion.

At the time of this decision, the company had 3 trainee engineers who were about to complete their training period of one year within a month. When they were asked to apply for this post, only one of them, Shailesh Deshmukh, the trainee engineer who had joined as assistant engineer in design department wanted to continue in the company. The other two engineers wanted to join some other company. To fill up these posts, the company released an advertisement in the local newspaper as per the recruitment policy.

Raju, a diploma engineer, who was working in quality assurance for the last ten years, was interested in applying for the above post of assistant engineer. He had joined as a supervisor but because of his good performance, he was promoted twice and presently he was working as senior supervisor in the quality assurance department.

The advertisement issued in the newspaper got a good response. The human resources department after going through the applications chose three candidates for the final interview. Raju met his superior, Amit Kumar, and expressed his desire to apply for the post. Amit Kumar suggested his name to the plant head. The plant head knew Raju very well, so he asked HR department to call him for an interview. He further told Amit Kumar that Raju, however, would have to pass all the tests and interviews like the other candidates.

Raju along with the three other engineers appeared for tests and interview. He scored well as compared to the other three candidates. The plant head was the head of the interview panel and he decided to select Raju for the post. Amit Kumar congratulated Raju for his success. However, after two days, Raju came to know that the engineer who was shortlisted next was selected for the post.

When asked, Raju was told that –

(a) The post required a degree and he was a diploma holder.

(b) The company did not want to lose a competent person from quality assurance department, which was a very fundamental function as regards its product.

Raju, however, was not satisfied with the reply he received from the management.

Questions

1. As per your opinion did the management make a mistake in calling Raju for an interview? Did he deserve the job?

2. What suggestions would you give to improve the recruitment process with reference to the above situation?

Case 2: Efficiency of Selection Process vis-a-vis Labour Turnover

Reylon is an insurance company with branches all over India. All the HR tasks of the firm are performed by the HR professionals that are based in the headquarters of the firm situated in New Delhi. The hiring practice of the firm is that the HR staff at the central office recruits the employees for the managerial team for all its branches and leaves the recruitment of other teams to the managers responsible for their own branches. In recent times, the firm opened a branch at Rameswaram in Tamil Nadu.

Amitabh, General Manager (HR), posted Arvind as the manager for the branch that was opened recently. In conformity with the firm's hiring practice, Arvind recruited other employees for his branch. But within one year of its business, this branch saw a high labour turnover. The turnover rate was much higher than the firm's general average of 10 percent. Posts like accounts officer turned over four times while computer operators worked only for a few months and this was the case, with the salespeople, who, in general, survived only for a few months. The head office seriously considered these developments.

The branch manager was called to the HR department of the head office to explain the reason for such a high labour turnover in his office. Amitabh, the HR general manager asked Arvind about the hiring practices implemented for selecting employees for his branch. In the beginning, Arvind explained that he made an evaluation of the candidates based on the information given by them in their application forms. Those who met the least criteria set for the job were called for an unstructured interview. All through the interview, the candidates were asked questions that were related to their profession to determine their knowledge, skill and expertise in the job.

Arvind stated that he observed the candidate's sitting posture, how he presented himself, his early remarks, his mannerisms and also his clothing. These factors had an important influence on his final evaluation of the candidate. The candidate was also quizzed about his real objective for joining this firm and also his career plans. Ultimately, a list based on the interview performance was made and the job offer given to the selected applicants.

Amitabh, who listened carefully to Arvind, was neither satisfied nor dissatisfied with Arvind's description but started thinking seriously about the possible role of the selection process in contributing to the high labour turnover.

Questions:

1. What is your opinion of the hiring policy followed in Reylon?
2. What is your assessment of the hiring practices adopted by Arvind?
3. State the recommendations you would make to Arvind for improving his hiring practice.

***

Case 3: Ethics in Head Hunting

Sunrise Steel Works (SSW) is a rerolling mill located near Jamshedpur which by melting iron changes it into blooms, rods and wires. As the construction industry in the country is thriving, there is a good demand for usable steel producers like SSW with its rerolling method. It is capable of competing well with major steel plants like SAIL and TISCO.

SSW has made a decision to develop the plant at Jamshedpur and obtained the plant and equipment that is required. It is searching for an experienced metallurgical engineer with blast furnace experience in major steel plants to lead its operations.

SSW has demanded the services of a head hunter firm (HHF) to concentrate on Visakhapatnam Steel Plant to poach a few of its experienced metallurgical engineers. SSW gave a sign that it would pay a minimum fifty percent more of what the candidate was currently getting which could go up to one hundred percent for a worthy candidate. Usually Indians are homesick and would like to have a job that is closer to their homes or at least in the same state they come from. Cashing on this attitude, SSW wanted candidates that came from Bihar or West Bengal to get attracted to a job that was closer to home. HHF demanded that SSW must pay one month's salary as service charges if a candidate is selected and joined service. If no candidate joined, then SSW should meet HHF's administrative costs on the real cost.

HHF began its hunting and ultimately found six engineers of Visakhapatnam Steel Plant who estimated SSW's requirement. HHF sent short resumes of these six candidates to SSW whose CMD selected three out of six and asked HHF to concentrate on them. HHF made contacts with those three candidates over phone and said that an attractive job as Head of Operations was waiting and if they are interested they must come for introductory briefing at a chosen local star-hotel. Each candidate met the head hunter alone and obtained full briefing about the job description and organisation profile. One candidate, after studying the profile of the firm, did not show any interest. Another candidate, Mukherjee, was interested only if the job was offered at its 24 Parganas plant. After confirming with the chiefs, the candidate was given a promise of posting in West Bengal after one year service at Jamshedpur plant. But this did not make the candidate happy and he too dropped out.

The third candidate, M. K. Dubey, was interested and began negotiating for better terms. After two rounds of discussion, the head hunter arranged a meeting between the Deputy Managing Director of SSW and Dubey at a star hotel in Visakhapatnam. After prolonged negotiations a high salary was set. Perks like furnished housing, company car and medical facilities were provided. Interest-free vehicle loan was promised for buying a car after one year of service. The job was on a 3-year contract which could be prolonged. Dubey was happy with the terms but said that he would like to visit the Jamshedpur plant and that he would need three months time to give notice to his current employer. SSW arranged return rail ticket to visit the plant and offered to compensate three months pay if the candidate decided to join work early at Jamshedpur.

Dubey visited the plant but was quiet for over two weeks. SSW was impatient to know when Dubey would join work. Dubey at last broke the news; he was not interested in the offer, which was communicated to SSW. The motives for turning down a lucrative offer were surprising. Dubey reasoned that (a) though he was from Bihar, the law and order condition was not good in the state and he had a quiet life at Visakhapatnam (b) the SSW factory was located some 35 km from Jamshedpur (c) there was no housing facility at plant site (d) above all there was no guarantee of job security (e) he was happy at Visakhapatnam Steel Plant where he was given housing, school was very near, good playgrounds, recreation centre good medical facilities, there was no narrow-mindedness or favouritism in the organisation, cost of living was relatively cheap. Overall the quality of life was good at Visakhapatnam Steel. This would adequately set of the rewarding increase in salary.

Questions

1. How did the company lure its engineers towards Visakhapatnam Steel?
2. According to your opinion how should the company recruit employees?

Case 4: Recruitment in Tesco

Tesco is the largest private sector company in the UK. Globally, the firm has more than 360,000 employees. In the UK, Tesco stores start from small local Tesco Express sites to big Tesco Extras and superstores. Around 86 percent of all sales are from the UK.

Tesco also works in 12 countries outside the UK, including China, Japan and Turkey. The firm has just opened stores n the United States. This international growth is part of Tesco's strategy to branch out and expand the business.

In its non-UK operations Tesco builds on the strengths it has developed as market leader in the UK supermarket sector. On the other hand, it also provides for local requirements. In Thailand, for instance, customers are used to shopping in 'wet markets' where the goods are not packed. Tesco uses this technique in its Bangkok store rather than providing pre-packaged goods as it would in UK stores.

- Tesco needs people across an extensive variety of both store-based and non-store jobs.
- In stores, it needs checkout staff, stock handlers, supervisors plus many specialists, such as pharmacists and bakers.
- Its distribution depots need people skilled in stock management and logistics.
- Head office provides the infrastructure to run Tesco well. Roles here consist of human resources, legal services, property management, marketing, and accounting and information technology.

Tesco aims to make certain all roles work together to drive its business goals. It needs to make certain that it has the right number of people in the right jobs at the right time. To achieve this, it has a structured process for recruitment and selection to attract candidates for both managerial and operational jobs.

Recruitment involves attracting the right candidates to apply for vacancies. Tesco advertises jobs in different ways. The process differs depending on the job available.

Internal recruitment

Tesco first looks at its internal Talent Plan to fill a vacancy. This is a process that lists existing employees looking for a change, either at the same level or on promotion. If there are no appropriate individuals in this talent plan or developing on the internal management development programme, for a fortnight, Tesco advertises the post within on its intranet.

External recruitment

For external recruitment, Tesco advertises vacancies through the Tesco website www.tesco-careers.com or through vacancy boards in stores. Applications are made online for managerial positions. The selected candidates have an interview followed by attendance at an evaluation centre for the final stage of the selection process.

People who are interested in store-based jobs with Tesco can approach stores with their CV or register though Jobcentre Plus. The store makes a waiting list of individuals applying in this manner and calls them in as jobs become available.

For harder-to-fill or more specialist jobs, such as bakers and pharmacists, Tesco advertises externally –

• Through its website and offline media.

• Through television and radio.

• By placing advertisements on Google or in magazines such as The Appointment Journal.

Tesco will look for the most cost-effective way of drawing the right applicants. It is costly to advertise on television and radio, and in some magazines, but at times this is required to guarantee the right type of people get to hear about the vacancies.

Tesco makes it simple for candidates to learn about jobs that are available and has an easy application process. By accessing the Tesco website, a candidate can learn about local jobs, management posts and head office positions. The website has an online application form for people to submit directly.

Questions

1. Analyse this case and comment on the recruitment process.
2. Give solutions on how Tesco can apply or use better selection or recruitment techniques.

***

Case 5: You Call this Selection!

Suresh Kumar was production manager for Singer Industries Limited, a Noida based electrical appliances firm near Delhi. Suresh had to approve the hiring of new supervisors in the plant. The HR manager carried out the first screening.

On Friday afternoon, Suresh got a call from Anil Dhavan, Singer's HR Director. 'Suresh' Anil said, "I have just talked to a young engineering graduate from a regional engineering college who may be just who you're looking for that supervisor job you asked me about. He has some good work experience in a multinational company situated in Pune, but at a lower salary level; he wants to visit Noida where his parents live.' Suresh replied, "Well, Anilji, I would take care of the boy". Anil continued, 'He is here right now in my office. I am sending him to you, if you are free'. Suresh hesitated a moment before replying, "Great Sir. I am surely busy today but I can't afford to annoy you either. Sir, please send him at once".

A moment later, Ranga Rao, the new candidate arrived at Suresh's office and introduced himself. 'Come on in Rao', said Suresh. 'I'll be right with you after I make a few urgent phone calls". Fifteen minutes later, Suresh finished the calls and started interviewing Rao. Suresh was fairly impressed. The merit certificates, the best suggestion award from the previous multinational company and Rao's quick answers revealed the candidate's potential. In the meantime, Suresh's door opened and a supervisor yelled, 'We have a small problem on line number 5 and need your help'.

"Sure", Suresh replied, "Excuse me for a minute Rao". After fifteen minutes, Suresh returned and the conversation continued for another few minutes before a series of phone calls again interrupted him.

The same pattern of interruption continued for the next forty minutes. Rao looked at the watch uncomfortably and said, "I am sorry Suresh. I have to go now. I have to catch the train to Pune at 9 p.m.".

"Sure thing, Rao", Suresh said as the phone rang again, "Call me after a week".

Questions

1. What specific policies might a company follow to avoid interviews like this one?

2. Explain why Suresh and not Anil should make the selection decision.

3. Is it a good policy to pick up candidates through 'employee referral method'? Why? Or why not? Explain keeping the case in the background.

✱✱✱

Case 6: What is more important – Recruiting or Retaining?

Uptron Electronics Limited is a new and internationally reputed company in the electronics industry and one of the biggest companies in the country. It attracted employees from internationally reputed establishments and industries by providing high salaries, bonus, etc. Just recently it has advertised for position of an electronics engineer. Nearly 150 candidates applied for the job. Sashidhar, an electronics engineering graduate from Indian Institute of Technology with 5 years working experience in a medium-sized electronics company, was selected from among the 130 candidates who took tests and interviews. At his request, the interview board suggested an improvement in his salary by ₹ 5,000 more than his current salary. Sashidhar was very happy to attain this and was praised by several people including his earlier employer for his brilliant interview performance and wished him good luck.

Sashidhar joined Uptron Electronics Ltd. on 21st January, 2012, with great interest. He also found his job to be fairly secure and a challenging one and he felt it was highly important to work with this firm during the formative years of his career. He found his managers as well as subordinates welcoming and helpful. But this environment did not survive long. After one year of his service, he gradually learnt about numerous unpleasant stories about the firm, the management, the superior-subordinate relations, rate of employee turnover, particularly at higher level. However, he had promised many things to the management in the interview, and he decided to stay. He wanted to make the management happy through his hard work, firm commitment and devotion. He began maximising his contributions and the management got the impression that Sashidhar had settled down and will stay in the firm.

After sometime, the superiors began harassing Sashidhar. He was over-loaded with diverse jobs. His freedom in determining and implementing decisions was decreased. He was ill-treated on several occasions before his subordinates. His colleagues also began assigning their responsibilities to Sashidhar. As a result, there were imbalances in his family life, social life and organisational life. But he seemed to be calm and satisfied. The management felt that Sashidhar had the potential to bear by many more organisational responsibilities.

So the general manager was much taken aback to see the resignation letter of Sashidhar along with a cheque equal to a month's salary one fine morning on 18th January, 2014. The general manager was unsuccessful in convincing Sashidhar to remove his resignation and relieved him on 25th January, 2014. The general manager wanted to appoint a committee to go into the matter at once, but dropped the idea later.

Questions

1. What prevented the general manager from appointing a committee?
2. What is wrong with the recruitment policy of the company?
3. Why did Sashidhar's resignation surprise the general manager?

Case 7: Importance of Assumptions

Gain Chan Verma is the chief executive of a company at Ranchi in Orissa. Verma, after significant considerations, decided that he urgently required a brilliant specialist in marketing management. He sent for Barua, the personnel manager and explained to him his need for a brilliant marketer. Verma briefed Barua for about twenty-five minutes. The chief gave details about the traits he expected in a candidate for this post. Barua was directed to –

1. Release an advertisement, stating the last date for the receipt of the applications to be twenty-one days after the appearance of the advertisement.
2. It was decided that Barua will put on to a table the details of all the applications received and forwarded to Verma.
3. The personnel manager was recommended to select three worthy candidates. A note on each of the short-listed candidates along with original application was to be put up to Verma.
4. All the staff work relating to the vacancy should be finished within the time period of 2 months.

Verma was pleasingly amazed when on the fifty-ninth day of the meeting with Barua two folders arrived from the personnel department. One folder enclosed chart details of all the twenty-six applications received and the other enclosed the article and applications of the selected three candidates. The chief opened the folder of the shortlisted candidates and hoped that the selection could be finished by examining the articles of the short listed candidates alone. He had requested the papers only as a standby measure and would see these only if selection could not be finished using the articles of the shortlisted candidates alone. The article was for 4 and not 3 shortlisted candidates. This was as follows –

Sunil Kumar Mitra is thirty-one years old. He has done his MBA in Marketing, from a famous university in UK and obtained 59.8 percent. He has been working in Manchester, UK for the last 6 years as a marketing executive. He has married an English lady and is ready to return to India, if he gets an appropriate opening in this country, preferably in eastern India.

Santam Das is twenty-six years old. He passed with first class in MBA, Marketing from the last batch of the Management Institute at Ranchi. He has done some short-term teaching projects since his results were declared. He has several offers for jobs but has not decided on his future course of action, because he is very fond of Ranchi and teaching.

P. S. Gill is twenty-nine years old. He has done his MBA in Marketing from Delhi University with an "A" grade. He has four years of experience in marketing of consumer goods in the rural markets in Punjab. He has firmly stated that he will not work for a pay package of less than ₹ 3 lakhs per annum.

A. N. Sinha is thirty-five years old. He is a senior clerk in the marketing section of our own company from the last fifteen years. He has extensive experience about all the events that have occurred in the profession of marketing in our company. He is intelligent, sincere and hard working. He does not fulfil the qualifications laid down for our project, but his name has been incorporated in the shortlisted candidates as a special enclosure. Sinha will be happy if he is promoted in acknowledgement of his contributions to the organisation and will be happy with a minor increase in his pay package. He need not be given the grades that will probably be demanded by other candidates.

Verma impressed by the short listing and write-up work of Barua, decides to finish the selection of the candidate without opening the folder of twenty-six tabulated applications. He reads the withdrawals of the shortlisted candidates one more time and keeps these papers in the pending tray thereafter. He wants to absorb this data and take an appropriate decision.

Questions

1. Give a solution to how Verma should select his candidates?
2. According to you who fits the criteria well and who should be selected? Justify.

Case 8: How Google Chooses Employees

Finding the best engineers, programmers, and sales representatives is a challenge for any firm, but it's particularly hard for a firm rising as fast as Google. Recently, the firm has doubled its ranks every year and has no plans to slow its hiring. More than 100,000 job applications pour into Google every month, and staffers have to sort through them to fill as many as 200 positions a week.

Near the beginning, the firm narrowed the pool of applicants by setting a very high standard on conventional measures such as academic success. For instance, an engineer had to have made it through school with a 3.7 grade-point average. Such criteria helped the firm find a convenient number of applicants to interview, but no one had really thought about whether they were the most suitable way to foresee success at the firm. More recently, the firm has attempted to apply its quantitative excellence to the problem of making better selection decisions. First, it set out to calculate which selection criteria were significant. It did this by carrying out a survey of employees who had been with Google for at least five months. These questions addressed an extensive range of features, such as areas of technical expertise, workplace behaviour, personality, and even some non-work habits that might reveal something significant about candidates. For instance, subscribing to a particular magazine or owning a dog could be connected to success at Google by ultimately measuring some significant feature no one had thought to ask about. The results of the survey were compared with measures of performance that were successful, including performance appraisals, compensation, and organisational citizenship.

One significant lesson of this effort was that academic performance was not the best forecaster of success at Google. No single factor forecasted success at every job, but a combination of factors could help in predicting success in specific positions. From this information, Google compiled a set of questionnaires that were connected to success in specific types of work at Google – engineering, sales, finance, and human resources. Now people who apply to work at Google go online to answer questions such as 'Have you ever started a club or recreational group'and 'Compared to other individuals in your peer group, how would you explain the age at which you first got into computers on a scale from 1 [much later than others] to 10 [much earlier than others]'? The information is analysed by a series of formulas that calculate scores from 1 to 100. The score forecasts how well the applicant is expected to fit into the kind of position at Google. Michael Mumford, an expert in talent evaluation at the University of Oklahoma, says that, generally, this approach to forecasting performance is efficient, but only when it depends on rational measures. So, starting a club might be a way to compute leadership behaviour, but owning a dog should be used only if the employer can find a description for why it is important.

Questions

1. Based on the information given, would you say that Google's use of questionnaires is a reliable, valid, and generalisable way to select employees? Why or why not?
2. How does this approach to selection contribute to making selection decisions that avoid illegal discrimination?
3. Besides the questionnaires, what other selection methods would you recommend that Google use? How would these improve selection decisions?

2.2 Training and Development

Case 1: Tata Sky

Tata Sky is a satellite television provider that has revaluated the television viewing experience for thousands of families across India. The service aims to give power to the Indian viewer with choice, control and convenience through its extensive collection of programming choices and interactive characteristics offered in DVD quality picture and CD quality sound. The firm is a joint undertaking between the Tata Group and the Star Group and works under the Sky brand owned by British Sky Broadcasting.

Problem: Tata Sky was growing and racing to keep up. The firm, a combination of Indian behemoth Tata Group and Britain's Sky television brand, was the second company in India to offer direct-to-home satellite television and other services. After two years of quick growth, management wanted more speed, but administration and disagreements were restraining efficiency.

"Because we are neither just entertainment nor telecom nor consumer household, we have individuals with backgrounds in different industries and very different working styles," said Charanjit Lehal, senior training manager. "Nobody was speaking the same language, and it was affecting efficiency—we could see a pattern of meeting after meeting, and quick decisions were not being made."

Executives observed the following types of behaviours –

- People avoided each other rather than confronting problems.
- Employees returned from meetings with other functions criticising about the list of impractical projects they were being asked to complete.
- Team problems were being escalated to high-level executives instead of being resolved at a previous stage.

The Training Course: After searching dozens of training courses, the Tata Sky learning and development team led by Bhaskar Bhattacharya, vice president of learning and development, directed three different workshops that were carried out by external trainers. On the basis of feedback and results, they chose to go forward with VitalSmarts Crucial Conversations Training. Lehal found the skills taught in the course were understandable. The tests and exercises were helpful in involving participants. He also liked how the action items required by the course helped each participant customise the principles to their particular requirements. On the basis of the course's value, Lehal was capable of securing executive approval by showing how the results would cause a return on investment. Besides the results and the skills, Lehal found the training flawlessly incorporated across cultures. There was no cultural misunderstanding between the American-based course and Tata Sky's Indian employees. "Dialogue is a necessity for any conversation," Lehal said. "The core content of the course has universal application."

He accepted that, speaking in general; Americans may be direct in conversations while people from eastern cultures may build more background before coming to a main point. "While methods vary, we still need to get on the table about what you are trying to say and what I am trying to say, and that is what this course teaches," he said. Lehal's experience was that with adequate preparation cultural differences did not present important challenges. On the basis of a suggestion from a VitalSmarts master trainer, he also investigated participants before they joined the course and developed real-life examples for use in the course from their unknown replies. This guaranteed immediate application to their work environment. Lehal conducted two-day workshops at each of Tata Sky's four regional offices, concentrating on the customer service function before moving to other functions.

Results: Tata Sky is observing the change in behaviour they wished for after improving its managers' communications skills. "This course is breaking down passive or aggressive cultures that had been found in different divisions," Lehal said. "It's become a very successful culture-building intervention."

Some results from the training –

- Two teams had been struggling to work together. One said that the other had been "moving to silence" and holding back their opinion, but is now "stepping up to important conversations."

- One manager told Lehal when she came into the training that she was searching for a new job because she was being made a scapegoat in her team. She was in "complete silence mode" and shunning the problem. After the training she talked to her supervisor about it and is still with the firm.

- The head of a service function was so impressed by the word-of-mouth on the course among his managers that he asked Lehal to conduct it for his senior team of general managers and vice presidents.

On an individual level, employees have shared with Lehal that the course has helped them sort out communication issues.

Questions
    1.   What were the problems that troubled Tata Sky?
    2.   Analyse and suggest different training methods that could be used in Tata Sky.

***

Case 2: Case Study of Nestlé – Training and Development

Introduction: Today, Nestlé is the world's leading food firm, with a 135-year history and companies in almost every country in the world. Nestlé's main assets are not office buildings, factories, or even brands. Rather, it is a global organisation that consists of many nationalities, religions, and ethnic backgrounds all working together in one single unifying corporate culture.

Training Programs at Nestlé: The readiness to learn is thus an important condition to be used by Nestlé. First and foremost, training is done on-the-job. Guiding and training is part of the duty of each manager and is important to make each one develop in his/her position. Formal training programs are usually purpose-oriented and designed to develop related skills and competencies. Therefore they are suggested in the framework of personal development programs and not as a reward.

Literacy Training: Most of Nestlé's people development programs assume that the employees are well educated. On the other hand, in numerous countries, we have decided to offer employees the chance to improve their literacy skills. Several Nestlé firms have thus arranged special programs for those who, for one reason or another, missed a big part of their basic schooling.

These programs are particularly significant as they introduce refined production methods into each country where they work. As the level of technology in Nestlé factories has gradually increased, the need for training has risen at all levels. Much of this is on-the-job training to improve the specific skills to operate more superior tools. But it's not only new technical abilities that are needed but also new working practices. For instance, more flexibility and more independence among work teams are at times required if the equipment is to function at maximum efficiency. "Sometimes we have debates in class and we are afraid to stand up. But our facilitators tell us to stand up because one day we might be in the parliament!" (Maria Modiba, production line worker, Babelegi factory, Nestlé, South Africa).

Nestlé Apprenticeship Program: Apprenticeship programs have been an important part of Nestlé training where the young trainees spend three days a week at work and two at school. Due to these programs there were positive results but some of these soon ran into a problem. At the end of training, several students were employed by other firms which gave no training of their own.

Local Training: Two-thirds of all Nestlé employees work in factories, most of which organise continuous training to meet their particular requirements. Besides that, numerous Nestlé operating firms run their own residential training centres. The result is that local training is the biggest part of Nestlé's people development activities worldwide and a considerable majority of the firm's 2,40,000 employees get trained every year.

Guaranteeing suitable and continuous training is an official part of every manager's responsibilities and, in several cases, the manager is personally engaged in the teaching. For this purpose, part of the training structure in every firm concentrates on developing the managers' own teaching skills. Extra courses are held outside the factory when needed, usually related with the operation of new technology.

The programs that are held in Nestle are wide-ranging. They continue the training of ex-apprentices who have the potential to become supervisors or section leaders, and continue through many levels of technical, electrical and maintenance engineering plus IT management. The degree to which factories develop "home-grown" specialists differs significantly, reflecting the availability of trained people on the job market in each country. On-the-job training is also an important part of career development in commercial and administrative positions. Here too, most of the courses are delivered in-house by Nestlé trainers but, as the level increases, partnership with outside establishments increases.

Almost every national Nestlé firm organises management training courses for new employees with high school or university qualifications. But their approaches differ significantly. In Japan, for instance, they include a series of short courses that lasts three days each. Subjects consist of human evaluation skills, leadership and strategy plus courses for new supervisors and the new staff. In Mexico, Nestlé established a national training centre in 1965. Besides those following regular training programs, some 100 people follow programs for young managers there every year. These are on the basis of a series of modules that permit customised courses to be offered to each individual that is taking part. Nestlé Pakistan runs 12-month programs for management trainees in sales and marketing, finance and human resources, and in milk collection and agricultural services. These involve periods of fieldwork, not only to develop an extensive variety of skills but also to introduce new employees to the organisation and systems. The scope of local training is getting bigger. The growing knowledge with information technology has allowed "distance learning" to be an important resource, and several Nestlé firms have employed corporate training assistants in this area. It has a big advantage of enabling students to select courses that meet their personal requirements and do the work at their own speed and suitable time. In Singapore, to quote just one example, the staff is given financial help to take evening courses in job-related subjects. Fees and expenses are effectively compensated, following courses leading to a trade certificate, a high school diploma, university entrance qualifications, and a bachelor's degree.

International Training: Nestlé's success in growing local firms in each country has been highly influenced by the performance of its international training centre, located near the firm's corporate headquarters in Switzerland. For over 30 years, the Rive-Reine International Training Centre has brought together managers from around the globe to learn from senior Nestlé managers and from each other. Country managers determine regarding who attends which course, although there is central screening for qualifications, and classes are carefully composed to incorporate people with a range of geographic and functional backdrops. Normally a class contains 15-20 nationalities. The centre brings some 70 courses that are attended by about 1700 managers each year from over 80 countries. All course leaders are Nestlé managers with several years of experience in various countries. Only 25 percent of the teaching is done by outside experts, as the main faculty is the Nestlé senior management. The programs can be largely divided into two groups.

Management courses: These account for about 66 percent of all courses at Rive-Reine. The participants have been with the company for four to five years. The intention is to develop a real admiration of Nestlé values and business approaches. These courses concentrate on internal activities.

Executive courses: These classes usually include people who have attended a management course five to ten years before. The focus is on developing the capability to represent Nestlé externally and to work with foreigners. It highlights industry analysis, often asking: "What would you do if you were a competitor?"

Conclusion: Nestlé's principle is that each employee should have the chance to develop to the maximum of his or her potential. Nestlé does this because they believe it pays off in the long run in their business results, and that continuous long-term relations with highly experienced people and with the communities where they work improve their ability to make consistent profits. It is significant to give people the chances for life-long learning as at Nestle that all employees are called to upgrade their skills in a fast-changing world. By providing opportunities to develop, they not only improve themselves as a firm, they also make themselves personally more autonomous, confident, and, in turn, more employable and open to new positions within the firm. Improving this circle is the final goal of their training efforts at many different levels through the thousands of training programs they run each year.

Questions

1. Analyse the different types of training methods used at Nestle.

2. Comment on the management's role in undertaking training workshops in the company.

***

Case 3: Is Satish in Need of Corrective Training?

Satish Sharma has been employed for six months in the accounts section of a big manufacturing firm in Faridabad. You have been his supervisor for the past three months. In recent times you have been asked by the management to learn about the contributions of each employee in the accounts section and monitor carefully whether they are meeting the standards set by you.

Only some days back you have finished your formal investigation and with the exception of Satish, all appear to be meeting the targets that are set by you. Along with a number of mistakes, Satish's work is characterised by low performance, usually he does 20 percent less than the other clerks in the department.

As you look into Satish's performance review sheets again, you start wondering whether some sort of remedial or corrective training is required for people like him.

Questions

1. As Satish's supervisor can you find out whether the poor performance is due to poor training or to some other cause?

2. If you find Satish has been inadequately trained, how do you go about introducing a remedial training programme?

3. If he has been with the company for six months, what kind of remedial programme would be best?

4. Should you supervise him more closely? Can you do this without making it obvious to him and his co-workers?

5. Should you discuss the situation with Satish?

***

Case 4: A Case on Training

Prateek Kumar, a manager with Systems Infotech, a leading management consultancy firm at Gurgaon, had been working in the firm for the last 14 years. During the 14 years of his service in the firm, he had not only trained many young managers but also provided guidance to them for their development. However, he observed that almost all of them left the firm as soon as they had found a better opportunity in some other company. Many of them had even undergone some specialised training which was sponsored by Systems Infotech.

Being a consultancy firm, Systems Infotech had a very fair policy as regards education wherein 80% costs of the tuition fee and books were reimbursed by the company. Many new engineers and officers took advantage of these educational opportunities.

Snehal Chatterjee had joined the Human Resource Department as a Junior Officer. She took this opportunity and completed her MBA. She had received almost ₹ 2 lakhs as reimbursement through the Company's education assistance programme. On hearing this, Prateek Kumar congratulated Snehal on her success.

However, a few days later, Prateek met Snehal for some official work. During their conversation, it transpired that Snehal had decided to resign in a couple of days and was planning to join their competitor firm at New Delhi. The reason for the same was attributed to the lack of prospects as regards growth in Systems Infotech.

After hearing this, Prateek Kumar became very upset and angry as this thing had been happening quite frequently during the last couple of years. Therefore, he decided to take up this matter with the director of the company. He met the director in this regard and briefed him on the issue of company's reimbursement policy and its lack of accountability.

Questions:

The director called the HR manager and asked to revise the policy, in such a way as to ensure that it creates value for the company's human resources.

1. Can you identify the reasons for employees leaving the company after enhancing their qualification?

2. If you are an HR manager, what would you do to handle the aforesaid situation? What changes would you suggest to the director?

***

Case 5: A Case Study on Training

One Monday morning, Sanjay Nagpal, an employee who was just recently recruited from a reputed management institute in Manipal walked into the sales office at Chennai as a new sales trainee. Raghavan, the zonal sales manager for a big computer hardware company was there to greet him. Raghavan's job included supervising the work of sales officers, field executives and trainee salesmen figuring over 50 of three areas of Chennai, Bangalore, and Trivandrum. The sales growth of employer's parts and other office equipment in his area was very satisfactory, particularly in recent years, because of the developmental schemes taken by individual state governments in spreading computer education in offices, schools, colleges, banks and other establishments.

Raghavan had collected many sales reports, catalogues and pamphlets explaining in detail the types of office equipment sold by the firm. After a nice chat about their backgrounds, Raghavan gave Sanjay the gathered material and showed him to his allotted desk.

After that Raghavan excused himself and did not come back. Sanjay spent the entire day examining the material and at 5.00 pm he picked up his things and went home.

Questions:

1. What do you think about Raghavan's training programme?
2. What type of sales training programme would you suggest?
3. What method of training would have been best under the circumstances? Would you consider OJT (On-The-Job training) simulation or experiential methods?

Case 6: A Case on Training

Kaul started working for the Satnam Manufacturing Company (SMC) as a human resources department trainee a few days after he received his MBA degree in management from a big mid-western university in Maharashtra. After a one-year training programme he worked for two years as assistant director of training and development in one of SMC's big machining and assembly plants. He was promoted as a plant director of training and development, in which he worked for just four years. When this project ended, Kaul was relocated to corporate headquarters as a staff assistant to the corporate director of training and development but Kaul understood that this depended on how well he handled his first major project.

SMC was planning to open a new plant in 16 months. The new plant was to employ around 4,000 employees within three years. On the other hand, only one of the eight production lines was to function when the plant opened. The other seven would be opened during the following three years. Construction of the new plant had just begun in a small town of 10,000 individuals, 18 miles south of Sinnar, Nashik. The plant would be the same as the plant in which Kaul was asked to submit a plan for training the employees for the new plant. He was given four months to do the job.

The top management had made the decision that employees from its other 21 plants would be reassigned to fill all second-level and higher management positions. For the majority of these employees, it would be a promotion. Also, the majority of non-management employees in the firm would be offered jobs in the new plant but few were expected to accept. All the management must be trained by SMC, not hired "off-the-street".

Kaul had 16 months, including his planning time, to determine how to train a workforce of about 450 new employees. About 55 to 60 management employees would be relocated to the new plant when it opened. He also had to create plans for training employees for the expansion of the plant to 4,000 employees by the assignment's working date.

He was unsure of what he should do, as this was the first time the firm had ever built and staffed a new plant. There was no past experience on which way to go. He decided his first task was to recognise his major problems.

Questions

1. In general, what training should take place prior to the opening of the new plant in 16 months?

2. What training should take place between the time the plant opens and all eight production lines are in operation?

3. How many frontline supervisors had to be trained? And how were they to be trained?

***

Case 7: Loews Hotels: We Train to Please

'Chocolates on the pillows'; 'A bathroom floor you can eat off of'; 'Service with a smile'. When guests go to a hotel or resort, they want all the comforts of home, as well as being provided personalised service. Here is how Loews Hotels, Wequassett Resort and Golf Club and La Quinta Inns and Suites use training to mesmerise their customers and make them come back for more.

How does one live up to a brand promise? At Lowes Hotels, a luxury hospitality chain based in New York with 18 properties in North America, in cities such as Miami Beach, Denver, and Las Vegas, the brand promise is to deliver a "four diamond and more" experience is a large part of living up to that promise.

Training at all levels concentrates on how employees, whether one is a housekeeper, a bellman, or a marketing director, can help to deliver on that promise. With 8,000 line-level employees and 12,000 managers to keep up to speed, that's a big promise to keep. "It's about what we do for guests to make their experience memorable and make them want to come back to a Loews hotel", says Jenny Lucas, director of education and development for Loews.

This is comparatively new for the firm, which has changed its systems in several ways. It begins with the training department. Training managers at Loews are more like information managers. They don't use much of their time on formal training; rather, they work in the departments and develop a connection with the employees on the floor. They make department report cards every month to report on how performance is on the progress, and they use a lot of time in training.

"Classroom training is part of the puzzle, but without true behaviour change and responsibility, you haven't completed that puzzle", says Lucas. "So our training managers are out there, observing the training that is being delivered, observing managers in action, doing spot checks, and giving feedback afterward. They're the keepers of service and standards, so they have to be reachable and capture the knowledge of how operations work every day". Lucas indicates that 13 out of the 18 training managers were promoted from line-level jobs or from operations, so they personally understand the procedures and the culture.

For line-level employees, training communicates the service standards through the classroom. For instance, in a brand that promises class, employees study about the expectations of the company's culture. Classes consist of role-playing and imitations –

the live or videotaped kind, not the electronic kind. The immediacy of video or live role plays assists in driving the message home, and the group experience is a part of that. Although Lucas says the firm has interest in incorporating more technology with its training, for a lot of employees it just wouldn't seem sensible.

"Our managers are the only ones with computers, and one whole department might share a computer" says Lucas. 'This approach makes more sense on the basis of the content and resources we're expressing. We're looking at some technology-oriented content that wouldn't need a computer, such as podcasts, but we're not there yet".

At the management level Loews has nearly 1,200 core management workshops, a train-the-trainer program, and other management workshops like the one on building the brand assist in creating leadership that cannot only assist in developing the brand but inspire others to do so, as well.

Changes in the firm's performance management system also have made the brand promise more distinguished. The firm has created a system in which individual managers' performance ratings are connected to their contributions to the firm's goals.

The firm has also started to increase its own crop of quality employees, whose chances of rising in the firm are good because of their potential. The thought is to grow gifted leaders, but also to "raise" people who get the culture and who understand how to make a hotel feel like a Loews Hotel. Loews' high-potential program provides extra training, development planning, and additional chances to employees who show promise, and it is incorporated with the performance review process. Managers are asked what they're doing to develop their people, and the response s performance rating. A focus on growing its own has already become fruitful; internal promotions have been running at about 55 percent, and more than 75 percent of the former high-potential program individuals that are taking part were still with the firm and have been promoted.

"The program began with the focus on operations and the front desk employees, maintenance positions, and the ike," Lucas says, "But now all disciplines are in the program in different ways".

Going forward, Lucas would love to do more of the videos that assist in teaching front-line employees in good service, so that more specific visual examples of more tasks would be accessible. And although particular barriers limit the firm's use of technology-based learning, Lucas wants to move into offering more remedies of that kind on site.

She also wants to tap into the generation known as Y, and to do so, her department has been discovering the possibilities of MySpace. Loews is not really using it for training yet, but Lucas knows the way to Gen Y goes through avenues such as iPods, podcasts and MySpace. "There are opportunities there; we just have to figure how to tap into them", Lucas says.

Questions

1. What can you tell about how Loews assesses the need for employee training?

2. From what you read, what principles of learning do you believe are embedded in Lucas' programs?

3. Do you think Loews should actively work toward incorporating more e-learning methods into its training programs? Why or why not?

2.3 Working Conditions

Case 1: Deterioration of all Working Conditions in Clothing Company

Textiles and clothing was one of the manufacturing branches that was hit the hardest by the crisis. Production is strongly linked with international markets. The impacts of the disaster in this sector have been mostly negative regarding employment, wages and all of other working conditions. Normally, in this respect, is the firm 'Robsov Ltd.', a medium-sized private firm.

Strong decline in output

Production is mostly for export. The firm works with materials supplied by foreign clients and relies on assignments that come out of the country. For this purpose, the effects of the world crisis on the company's output showed up before in the country altogether. All through the recession, the company lost an important part of its foreign markets and output contracted by around 64 percent. Besides that, the firm encountered problems with financing because credit conditions in Bulgaria declined. This condition negatively affected the working conditions in the company.

Strong Negative effect on Employment and Wages

The total number of employees in 2008 was 135 employees. 80 percent of the employees were working on the basis of permanent contracts and the rest on temporary contracts. New employees are on temporary contracts with time duration of six months.

All work full-time. Compared with educational stats, most employees have finished secondary and elementary education. The company experienced a scarcity of qualified employees both before and throughout the recession.

The negative effect of the recession on employment has been equal to the fall in output. From the start of 2009, employment began to decline, falling as low as 75 employees in the most difficult period. Over a time of few months the number of employees reduced by over 44 percent. Most of those sacked were low-skilled employees.

Wages reduced for all categories of employees. In comparison to the pre-recession period, the average wage in the company fell by 44.4 percent (from 450 BGN in 2008 to 250 BGN in 2009). In this time, the initial wage in the firm also declined because of part-time work (from 240 to 150 BGN). Changes appeared in the wage structure. All additional payments, such as bonuses, were also cut.

Deterioration of Other Working Conditions

To save the remaining part of the personnel, the firm used flexible working time and unpaid leave. In the period January-June 2009, all employees moved to short-time working (four hours a day) and received wage compensation. The management also motivated low-skilled employees to take unpaid leave, up to a maximum of 45 days. As said by the management, all these measures could not stop employment and wage reductions.

Although the problem of low qualifications continues, the management did not try to solve it. The money spent on training and recruitment was cut. Health and safety provisions were very less because the available resources had been decreased.

Concluding Remarks

The case study show that companies that have been hit the hardest by the crisis have in general allowed working conditions to worsen. The employees in this clothing firm suffered from multiple negative effects because of the crisis. There were no trade-off effects between working conditions. The absence of social dialogue hampered any possible negotiated trade-offs. All working conditions declined to different degrees and this brought with it a greater inequality.

Questions

1. Analyse the working conditions of the clothing company
2. How can the management improve the conditions of the factory? Give few suggestions.

***

Case 2: Bharat Electronics Corporation Limited

Bharat Electronics Corporation Limited (BECL)'s sales go beyond ₹ 4500 million a year. Its countrywide operations employ about 38,000 people. BECL's product lines range from ₹ 12,000 electronic typewriters to data processing systems that sell for ₹ 11,00,000. It controls over 40 percent of the country's market for computing equipment. The firm in general is recognised to be one of the most flourishing and best-managed corporations in India. Obviously, it did not attain its importance solely on luck. The firm obviously does several things that work. The following describes a few of the qualities that make BECL the indisputable leader in its profession.

Employee behaviour at BECL is the product of its founder's philosophy. Dhiren Shah had rules for nearly everything. Dark business suits, white shirts, and striped ties were the "executive uniform". Drinking alcoholic beverages, even off the job, was strictly forbidden. Employees were expected to accept regular transfers. Today, the rules are a bit less harsh, but the traditional image is still there. Male sales employees are expected to wear suits and ties when meeting customers, but shirts no longer have to be white. All employees have to go through a 32-page code of business ethics.

BECL has always shown a strong commitment to its employees. Individuals at times get sacked, but it has never let go anyone to cut costs. Redundant employees are retrained and then re-allotted. But this commitment is two way: BECL carefully screens job candidates to recognise individuals who will grow with the firm. New employees are expected to spend their working careers with BECL. Of course, it does not always work that way. Several employees leave willingly as they are required in other firms for senior executive positions.

Salaries and benefits at BECL, are highly competitive. In many state units, the firm has its own staff quarters and recreation clubs and the membership is a meagre ₹ 5 a year. It is not surprising that this concern for its employees has led to strong committed personnel. BECL's success can be owed to its commitment to service. Its sales employees are systematically trained and well-informed. Most of the employees spend the better part of their first two months in classes that are run by the firm. Managers are needed to take at least sixty hours of additional instruction.

Every year, BECL spends more than ₹ 5 million on employee education and training. Customers are confident that if they have an issue with BECL equipment, its sales employees will be capable of solving them without any difficult procedure.

Commitment and service is strongly customer-focused. BECL spends a lot to obtain a complete and latest market research data on potential customer requirements. Contrary to many of its competitors, which have allowed technology to drive their product line. BECL wanted the customers to decide what it will produce and sell.

But maintaining a successful record also needs change. BECL has just shown that it can adapt to changing situations. Between 1986 and 1989, for faster innovation and flexibility, it established fifteen small independent units within the firm to look into such fields as robotics, specialised equipment, and analytical tools. Maybe its important departure from its past tradition has been connected to its commitment to compete in the personal computer market. The BECL PC is built mainly from parts bought from outside suppliers, making its technical requirements available to other companies so as to stimulate compatible software and peripheral equipment. The firm has even started to offer discount prices to stimulate sales.

Questions

1. Analyse the key issues discussed in the case.

2. Describe BECL's organisational structure and culture. Does this structure and culture inhibit (a) employee motivation, (b) employee innovation, or (c) organisational flexibility?

3. How do BECL's selection criteria, socialisation techniques, and reward system act to maintain its culture?

Case 3: A Case on Safety of Employees

Deccan Mechanical Works, an engineering company, supplies sub-assemblies to Indian Railways' coach building factory. A factory inspector recently visited the company for carrying out inspection as regards its safety and health provisions. This was the second visit by the factory inspector and, therefore, the director of the company requested permission from Bhosle, the factory inspector to take along with him Ajay Shinde, the personnel manager, during the walk-around. Shinde, although a new recruit, has a rich experience of six years in this field. Bhosle, however, asked the workers' representative also to accompany their staff. The report containing the following observations were submitted to the aforesaid company, after carrying out the inspection at sight:

1. Five temporary workers in the assembly shop were not wearing safety shoes, enquiries revealed that they were not provided for with the same.

2. No enclosures were provided in the welding section, thus, creating a situation whereby the arc light generated by continuous welding could be harmful to the workers' eyesight working in an adjacent space.

3. No medical register of the workers were available in the hazardous areas, which implies that the concerned workers may not have been examined for a long time.

4. Some of the workers working on heights were not properly safeguarded.

All these things were shown to Shinde and the worker's representative during the site inspection.

The firm provided their explanation for the above four points saying that:

1. They have already provided the safety shoes to their permanent employees, but as the new batch of temporary workers had joined just two days back, they would be providing them with the safety shoes within a day.

2. In the welding department, an enclosure was provided for, but it was removed by the workmen concerned as they felt that this made them feel very hot.

3. Medical check-ups were done regularly, but since the medical attendant concerned was on leave for that particular day, the medical officer could not produce the same.

4. For safety purposes the concerned workers were instructed and provided for with nylon nets, but they were not using them at the time of inspection.

After receiving the aforesaid reply, the factory inspector decided to plan an unscheduled surprise visit to confirm the justification submitted by the firm.

Questions

1. If you were the personnel manager, how would have you handled the situation? Do you agree with the reply given by the company?

2. Based on the observations made by the factory inspector, write your observations on safety and health compliance status existing in the company.

✳✳✳

2.4 Salary and Wage Administration

Case 1: Pareek Laboratories

Pareek Laboratories was founded in 1979 as a medium-sized pharmaceutical firm with just two common products and 340 employees. In a span of 30 years, it surprisingly expanded and now emerged as the second-best pharmaceutical firm in the country with a sizeable presence in the global market. The firm's staff list includes 8200 talented employees. Now, the firm has twelve research centres, of which four are located abroad. It is marketing nearly 625 branded products in more than 58 countries. On an average, it has also succeeded in launching 20 products in a year, which itself shows the strength of its human resources.

The top management of the firm strongly believes that its highly skilled employees are accountable for its astonishing performance and growth. The firm has a full-fledged HR department under the stewardship of HR director Nikesh Verma. The HR department, through constant measures and a thorough approach, has promoted loyalty and job involvement among the members of the company. Since its inception, the labour turnover rate of the firm has been far less than the industry average, except the past two years, including the present year.

Obviously, the firm is worried about the recent disturbing tendency in the employee attrition rate, predominantly at the executive levels. Since executive retention is important to the constancy of the business, the firm desires to decrease the executive turnover at the earliest before too much harm is done. Several executives have blamed the pay revision conducted two years back as accountable for this trend. In the last pay revision, the firm moved from a narrow-graded pay structure to a broad-graded one. As a result, the number of pay grades were decreased and kept to a minimum in the revised pay structure. Junior-level executives often complained that they got a raw deal in the new pay grade fixation and the pay difference between their level and the higher level executives became disappointingly big. The executives also found fault with the job assessment methods that are followed for determining the internal value of the jobs. They felt that the ranking technique adopted in job evaluation was highly biased and unpredictable. The junior-level executives also claimed that the job assessment committee had assessed individuals instead of positions at executive levels, and that was accountable for the anomalies in the pay grade distribution. They wanted the HR department to start a fresh and objective assessment of jobs and reallocate pay grades based on the result of a new job assessment.

On the other hand, the HR department, which takes complete responsibilities for job assessment and pay revisions, purposefully denied the accusations made by junior-level executives. It maintained that the job assessments were carried out in the most objective way. The HR people also said that the big differences between the pay scales of junior executives and those of the middle-level ones were because of a flow in the job assessment or pay revision process. But the junior-level managers were not ready to accept the explanation of the HR people and kept asking for a fresh exercise to fix the value of each job in the managerial levels and reallocate pay grades.

Now, the management has a severe problem. If it grants the request of the junior-level managers and orders a fresh job assessment and pay grade fixation for them, it might send wrong signals to other sections of the employees and they also might ask for revisions. If it does not grant their request, it will be impossible to decrease the high executive turnover. Ultimately, the management has instructed the HR department to come out with some reasonable solutions to this section issue.

Questions
1. Do you agree with the contention of the junior-level executives that flawed job evaluation and pay grade fixation are responsible for the labour turnover problems of the company?
2. According to you, who is to be blamed for the high level of executive attritions prevailing in the company?
3. If you were to be the HR director, how would you have responded to the criticism of the executives?
4. What will be your suggestions to solve the present imbroglio faced by the management?

Case 2: A Case on Wage Revision

Classic Paints is a manufacturing company established in 1970. The company is situated near Noida. The main product of the corporation is to produce and supply chemicals required to produce paints. They have collaboration with GHS Chemicals Corporation, London.

The plant has a 425 workforce, among these 110 are staff members and the rest are workmen. In the workforce most of the employees are chemists and engineers.

In recent times the management observed that the engineers' attrition rate was very high and most of the engineers were leaving the company in two or three years from the date of their joining. When the management analysed the attrition report they found out that the pay scale and working conditions were not appropriate as compared with their competitors.

With suggestions from the HR department they revised the pay structure of the engineer grade and also offered them other perks also like travelling allowance, a mobile and laptop with data card. Earlier, the difference in pay scale of chemists (science graduate) and engineers was about ₹ 5000 a month and with the revision in the pay the difference increased to ₹ 15,000 per month. This created a situation of ambiguity between the pay scale of the chemists with 10 to 12 years of experience and the engineers with 2 to 3 years experience.

The chemists presented their point of view to the management that their salaries also needed to be revised. The management explained to them that being a comparatively small corporation, and the small profit margin for the products, due to the competition. they could not consider their demand. The management insisted that the market value of engineers was higher so the management was compelled to pay higher salary to them as the company needed to have engineers to maintain the plant. However, the management decided to give a rise of ₹ 5000 per person to chemists to reduce the gap between the salaries of engineers and chemists.

However, the decision did not help much as it created de-motivation and dissatisfaction amongst the chemists. They did not take interest and responsibility in their work. The degree of cooperation between chemists and the engineers which was excellent earlier, had dipped and it was also observed that stoppages and breakdowns in the plant had increased. The blame game between chemists and engineers started as the work of machines maintenance was not done accurately. The chemists blamed the engineers and vice versa. These recurrent breakdowns of machines affected the profit of the company.

In such a situation the individual performance of the engineers also suffered poorly and they felt discouraged because in-spite of their working hard they were not able to deal with the increased breakdown frequency. The management also had concerns over the situation which also de-motivated the engineers and some of them chose to leave their company. The plant was also not able to achieve the normal level of output as maintained in the past, the management also showed their attitude to the new engineers as they were not maintaining the plant as was being done by the old engineers.

Points in the case

1. It was obvious that the company had to pay more to the new engineers because of market condition.

2. With this discrimination of difference in salaries the chemists began to feel frustrated.

3. Both the above reactions are expected and natural.

4. The management could not afford to increase the salary for everybody.

Questions

1. Analyse the wages that are given to the employees at Quality paints.

2. What were the disagreements between the management and the employees?

Case 3: A Case on Wage Grievance

The plant manager of ABC Corporation felt that the production of the factory would never come up to the management's expectations. One of the main causes he attributed to the same was the higher absenteeism. During the agriculture season, the workers of ABC Corporation did not attend to the factory because they had to farm their own lands. In many parts of India, the workman also happens to be a farmer; there is no shortage of food and his factory job only helps him in earning some additional cash money. As he is not totally dependent upon the factory wages, he does not take his duties seriously, and, therefore, resorts to frequent absenteeism, which becomes a cause of concern to the company.

About 6 years ago, in the farm equipment factory plant, a fruit processing unit was added by the company in the unoccupied place. The job in this unit was seasonal which lasted about 5-6 months in a year. The unit had 25 workmen, all in the category of semi-skilled workmen. They had installed two processing units.

One unit did the work of fruit cleaning, removing the skins, slicing, grading, storing, and packing operations. The other unit was generally used for extracting juices, processing and bottling operations. They had also provided machineries to prepare jams and pickles from the fruits. All these processed parts were kept in cold storage and then dispatched to different parts of the country as per the demand.

During the lean period, the major portion of workforce jobs came to an end, and the remaining workforce was transferred to the parent plant. However, a few workers continued with their jobs at the fruit processing unit. These activities involved loading of jam cartons and handling fruit packing, cleaning of the plant and machinery, and so on. However, manufacturing operations of the fruit jam and pickle work was constantly going on for all the seasons. The preparation of jam and pickles was not stopped as there was a continuous demand in the market. There were 5 operators who were working on these processes. Their trade was 'food processor' and they were trained in food processing for six months before joining this unit. Out of total 25 workmen, only 18 were permanent and others were temporary. These 5 workers were also from the permanent category. But they were not satisfied with their wages.

Their point was that their job was more of a continuous nature and required special skills; whereas others were having an easy time as compared to their work, yet they were being paid the same wages. Therefore, they demanded a revision of their grades and wages.

Their dissatisfaction was communicated to the HR manager of the unit concerned. He told them that, they could not be given higher grades even though they were doing a more skilled job as compared to the other workmen in the food processing unit, because the higher grade which they had demanded was allotted to the main unit workmen, who were SSC passed, ITI qualified operators. They were doing a job which required a higher skill level as compared to what these three workmen were doing.

The HR manager called all the 5 workers to his office and counselled them. However, they did not agree to take back their demand. After meeting with the HR manager, they resorted to a 'go slow' in their work. Many workmen were also on their side and felt that they should be paid more. Nevertheless, within the context of the entire unit, their demands could not be conceded.

Questions

1. As the personnel manager in the above case do you agree with the demands made by the three operators from the food processing unit? Give reasons to support your opinion.

2. As the personnel manager in the above case, what action would you suggest to the top management?

3. Can you find a solution without disturbing the present grade structure in the above case?

***

Case 4: Pay Status and Motivation

Change and Motivation

This mini-case study explores the motivational issues regarding pay and status differentials in the context of the management of change.

In a medium-sized NHS Trust Hospital in the UK all cleaning staff, nursing assistants and ward clerks formed a flexible, multi skilled, ward-based team of care assistants. Formal status and pay differentials between employees were decreased and many employees were upgraded and as a result received a basic pay rise. The new basic grade which applied to all care assistants decreased status differentials and simplified the bonus schemes that had developed. Some employees were asked to alter their shift pattern and the overall hours they worked within one week.

At the design stage, managers felt it would encourage the employees as all would 'feel part of a team'. This would, they believed, mainly apply to the domestics, who were usually not affiliated to a ward and as a result were remote from patients and from care assistant co-workers.

Pay Issue

One of the main issues that were discussed at the change project meeting before the implementation of the project was the pay scales that were recommended for these new roles. All employees would be classified as either Health Care Assistant (HCA1 - the lower scale) or HCA2 (the higher pay scale) and jobs would be evaluated to see into which group they fell; for example, those with supervisory duty would probably be classified as HCA2 and might be paid higher than HCA1 staff, regardless of whether they were an assistant nurse, ward clerk or domestic. All the employees would have protected pay for a year, that is, even if they were placed on a scale and job rate which was below their current pay, their income would not fall instantly.

Before implementation the HRM director argued, "What I'm interested in is whether the underlying principles are right, that is, are all the jobs, nursing (assistant), housekeeping and administration rated similarly, allowing for two grades of these personnel?". The chief executive, accountable to the Board of Directors for the Trust budget, proposed that he had some problems with the idea of thinking that these are all valued very similarly. "I instinctively would have put housekeeping at a lower level than administration and nursing; what I'm worried about is we're going to end up with the highest paid domestic personnel in the locality". The director of nursing interrupted, "It's very easy to drop back into 'old speak'. Why should people, just because they clean the toilet, be any different from those who make beds"?

Question

1.   Should cleaners be paid on the same scale as porters, administrators and nursing assistants?

2.   Discuss the motivational implications of these changes, drawing on theories and models presented in this case.

***

Case 5: A Case on Wage Increment

ABC Pvt. Ltd. is an electronics company with a workforce of 120 workers having an engineering division and an assembly division. The engineering division has a total workforce of 80 workers who are all male workers. The assembly division has a workforce of 40 women workers only. Almost all the workers are members of the MIDC workers union.

On 31st Dec. 2012, the last settlement on wages and working conditions signed between the management and the MIDC workers union had expired and the union had terminated that settlement and submitted a fresh charter of demands.

The present wages of the employees was as follows:

1. **Engineering Division**   :   Minimum - ₹ 18000 per month

                                   Maximum - ₹ 25000 per month

2. **Assembly Division**   :   Minimum - ₹ 12000 per month

                                   Maximum - ₹ 18000 per month

The union was demanding a rise of ₹ 1000 per month in the wages of all the 120 employees, and they were also demanding parity in the wages of the assembly division and the engineering division.

The personnel manager called the union office-bearers for negotiations and at the first meeting explained the basic premises on which negotiations will take place:

(a) Management is prepared to concede some wage rise to all the employees.

(b) Parity in the wages between engineering division and the assembly division cannot be agreed for the following reasons:

(i)   Work in both the divisions is not the same. Engineering division workers are paid more because of 'heavier work'.

(ii) Women workers of the assembly division are drawing one of the highest wages amongst women workers in the MIDC area.

The union office bearers argued that as both men and women workers are their members, they cannot practice discrimination.

Questions

1. As a personnel manager how would you prepare for the next round of negotiations?

2. What do you suggest as the solution to the above problem?

Case 6: Pay Decisions at Performance Sports

Katie Perkin's career goal while attending Rockford College was to get a degree in small business management and to start off her own business after graduation. Her last desire was to mix her love of sports and a strong interest in marketing to start a mail-order golf equipment business that was aimed particularly at beginner golfers.

In February 2003, after extensive planning and a loan in the amount of $75,000 from the Small Business Administration, Performance Sports was started. On the basis of a marketing plan that emphasised on fast delivery, error-free customer service and big discount pricing, Performance Sports grew quickly. At present the firm employs sixteen individuals – eight customer service agents each earning between $11.25 and $13.50 per hours, four shipping and receiving associates paid between $8.50 and $9.50 per hour; two clerical employees each earning $8.25 per hour; an assistant manager earning $15.25 per hour; and a general manager with a wage of $16.75 per hour. Both the manager and assistant manager are ex-customer service agents.

Perkins means to create a new managerial position, purchasing agent, to handle the difficult duties of buying golf equipment from the firm's many equipment manufacturers. Also, the mail-order catalogue will be extended to handle an entire line of tennis equipment. Since the position of purchasing agent is new, Perkins is not sure how much to pay to this individual. She wants to employ a person with five to eight years of experience in sports equipment purchasing.

While attending an equipment manufacturers' meeting in Las Vegas, Nevada, Perkins learns that a competitor, East Valley Sports, pays its customer service representatives on a pay-for-performance basis. Curious by this compensation philosophy, Perkins asks her assistant manager, George Balkin, to research the benefits and drawbacks of this payment strategy. This request has become important because only last week two customer service representatives conveyed their unhappiness with their hourly wage. Both criticised that they felt underpaid in relation to the big amount of sales revenue each produces for the firm.

Questions

1. What factors should Perkins and Balkin consider when setting the wage for the purchasing agent positions? What resources are available for them to consult when establishing this wage?

2. Suggest advantages and disadvantages of a pay-for-performance policy for Performance Sports.

3. Suggest a new payment plan for the customer service representatives.

2.5 Performance Management System

Case 1: Performance Management System: A Case Study of NTPC.

NTPC believes in attaining organisational excellence through human resources and follows the "people first" approach to control the potential of its 24,500 employees to its business plans. 'People before PLF (Plant Load Factor)' is the guiding philosophy behind the complete gamut of HR policies at NTPC. NTPC is strongly devoted to the development and growth of all its employees as people and not just as employees.

Elements of HR strategy: Competence building, commitment building, culture building and systems building are the four elements on which our HR systems are based. To accomplish HR and the corporate vision, an HR model has been developed by NTPC. As per the model, at the perimeter lies the role of HR to facilitate the organisation in completing its corporate social responsibility and facilitate good governance practices. Within this framework, lies the role of HR to set up good customer relationship. At the centre of the model, lies the role of HR to form a learning organisation on the basis of four elements that is building competence, commitment, culture and systems. All these HR roles are performed by a dynamic mechanism namely Systems Designer, Internal Consultant, Systems Monitor and Impact Assessors.

Performance Management System of NTPC: The focus of the performance management system for senior executives is to evaluate them on different elements of managerial responsibilities, including performance, generic managerial competencies, values and potential that add up to 100 marks. The performance component as recognised and measures that developed would have 50 percent weightage in total appraisal. Generic managerial competencies displayed by appraisees while performing duties have been given 20 percent weightage in appraisal. The firm's concern for materialisation of organisational core values is reflected in the performance management and is allocated a weightage of 15 percent in appraisal. The performance management system provides for appraisal of the executive's potential to presume that higher responsibility has a weightage of 15 percent in appraisal. The performance management system gets one's attention towards significant managerial attributes and strikes a balance between 'performance' and other aspects of managerial talents/skills. Executives will have a set of key performance areas to be recognised through discussion and attain them during the performance period. The system is to develop the competencies by engaging the executive in setting targets and recognising key performance areas. The system's objective is to bring the idea of ownership and responsibility on both appraisee and appraiser to generate mutual trust and confidence. To use the performance management system for facilitating personal career development and bring companywide HR interference at senior levels to link competency gaps.

Performance management system at NTPC includes appraisal of 5 components:

1. **Performance:** At NTPC, the performance is assessed at two intervals, that is, first half year performance appraisal, and second half performance appraisal.

    (a) **First Half Performance:** The system gives the reporting officer (appraiser) and the executive (appraisee) to recognise through discussion and choose a set of Key Performance Areas (KPAs) quickly at the start of the first half-year. While recognising KPAs, actual 'measures' for each KPA are defined in writing. The KPA targets are given different weightage and restricted to 8 key performance areas only. The plan is to allow the executive to concentrate on specified deliverables and not miss significant areas. The KPAs are determined using 'SMART' approach that is Specific, Measurable, Agreed, Realistic and Time-Bound. The appraiser and appraisee together develop KPAs, define measures and assign marks for each KPA at the start of first half year in April. The performance under Part IA is jointly reviewed and assessed at the start of 2nd half year. At the time of joint review, actual success is temporarily recorded against each KPA and marks obtained. Each KPA is shown in relevant column. The aggregate of marks obtained for different KPAs is worked out and shown as an aggregate of IA. Both appraisee and the reporting officer sign the Part IA.

(b) **Second Half Performance:** The system assists in reviewing the Key Performance Area targets for the second half year on the basis of the assessment of 1st half year KPAs depending on actual achievements. The reworked KPA targets are briefly recorded, 'measures' for each KPA defined and marks assigned. KPAs which expand beyond the 1st half year may be re-recorded in the targets of the 2nd half year.

2. **Competencies and Evaluation:** To reward appraisees, not only on the performance, but also on the competencies as performance may be influenced by many other factors on which the executive has no direct control. Competency-based evaluation would assist the organisation in taking systematic steps for linking the competency gaps.

(i) **Competencies:** There are 8 competencies evaluated and rated at NTPC. These competencies are Technical Knowledge, Business Attitude, Strategic Thinking, Resources Management, Communication Skills, Systematic Thinking, Interpersonal Competence, and Empowering Skills.

(ii) **Ratings and competencies:** The competencies are assessed yearly on a five-point rating scale – 1, 2, 3, 4 and 5 – the rating 1 being the lowest end of the scale and 5 being the highest on the scale. On the basis of the competencies observed, the reporting officer classifies each competency on a scale of 1 to 5. The reporting officer talks about each competency (A to H) with the appraisee and plans the rating. The competencies at the same time have a weightage of 20 percent in the total performance appraisal. The aggregate of the rating of each competency is to be reached at the bottom of the ratings column. After that, the aggregate rating is to be changed to marks out of 20 using the conversion formula. The Part II is accordingly signed by the appraisee and the reporting officer. The review of competencies and completion of Part II for the previous appraisal year is completed at the end of appraisal year, not later than 15th April.

3. **Values:** Adoption of the firm's core values in the business dealings is one of the important duties of employees at all levels. Particularly the senior executives who occupy

leadership positions in the firm, have an important role in the materialisation of core values by being 'role models' in observing and practising them and thus leading by example. Because of the stress laid on the core values shown by the executive in his everyday business dealings, 15 percent weightage has been credited in the performance appraisal to the process of value actualisation displayed by the executive.

(a) **Company values:** The corporate values 'COMIT' and the indicative observable behaviour regarding each value is customer focus, organisational pride, mutual respect and trust, initiative and speed, and total quality.

(b) **Ratings:** Each value has to be assessed through conversation on a rating scale of 1 to 5, the rating 1 being the lowest and 5 being the highest. The reporting officer would assess the appraisee on each of the values and mark the rating for each value. The ratings are then totalled at the bottom of the rating column out of a maximum of 25. The ratings acquired would be changed to 15 marks by the conversion formula given. The marks that are acquired out of 15 marks are written in the box. The Part III is signed mutually by the reporting officer and the appraisee. The assessment of values and completion of Part III for the preceding appraisal year is completed at the end of performance appraisal year, not later than 15th April.

4. **Potential Appraisal:** Potential is a part that is related to "competencies". It seeks to attain one of the main objectives of the performance appraisal system, namely assessing the appropriateness of the executive to presume higher responsibilities along the hierarchy. In due time, the appraisal of 'potential component' may be completed through the evaluation centre or with the aid of other means, to make the appraisal more sophisticated. The personality profile of each person based on the assessment centre or with the aid of other process can become accessible to the reporting officer to allow him to assess the potential of the appraisee with more impartiality. The reporting officer would neutrally assess the potential of the assessee based on factual information observed during the evaluation year.

(a) **Potential evaluation criteria:** The four basic competencies that are team-building, conceptual ability, strategic vision, and leadership abilities are covered for potential evaluation of executives.

(b) **Rating potential evaluation:** The evaluation of 'generic competencies' for potential appraisal is completed through conversation on a rating scale of 1 to 5, rating 1 is the lowest and rating 5 being the highest. The evaluation of potential is completed on each competency and rating given against each in the rating column by the reporting officer. The aggregate of all the competencies A to D would be reached by totalling all the ratings. This would be out of 20 marks. The potential appraisal has a weightage of 15 percent in the total performance appraisal. The rating on potential out of 15 marks is acquired by using the conversion formula at the bottom of Part IV. The marks that are acquired out of 15 marks are written in the box. The Part IV is mutually signed by the reporting officer and the appraisee at the bottom of the page. The appraisal of this part for the preceding appraisal year is completed at the end of performance appraisal year, not later than 15th April.

5. **Performance and Potential Profile:** The Part V would summarise all marks scored for the performance appraisal year. The marks scored for Part I, Part II, Part III and Part IV is moved to this section and entered against the particular item. The total of the marks scored is reached by adding all marks scored for different parts. This would form the final score of performance and potential appraisal rating of the executive out of 100 marks.

6. **Conclusion and Suggestion:** The performance management system is a tool to be used for recognising the developmental requirements of the appraisee. It is observed that performance management system of NTPC clearly knows what is to be achieved and developing the people to guarantee how it is to be attained. With an absolute clear vision and a strong HR strategy, its performance management system assesses its human resources on different parts of managerial responsibilities, including performance, generic managerial competencies, values and potential, reporting evaluates performance, competencies, values and potential. Hence, it is clearly based on study and evaluation of PMS system that the firm's appraisal system is strong enough to recognise and specifically address the developmental requirements so as to overcome the competency gaps in its human resources.

Questions

1. Why is a Performance Management System required in the company?
2. Analyse the Performance Management System used in NTPC.

✱✱✱

Case 2: E-mail Engineering Company India LTD.

A public limited company, E-mail Engineering Company, India, Limited is located in the foothills of Himachal Pradesh. The firm is a part of a big business house operating in the up country with its headquarters in Mumbai. The firm was founded in 1960s for manufacturing electronics/heavy engineering parts for the energy sector. The firm has about 9,000 employees. It is a profit-making firm.

The top management of the firm had changed hands three years ago. In 1999, the new CEO developed a turnaround strategy for the whole organisation. As such, the CEO had asked the head of HR to introduce performance management across the board as a medium for cultural change.

Corporate HR developed a Performance Management System (PMS) for the total organisation. The system was originally used as a pilot for a group of managers only for a year.

E-mail Engineering Company is famous for its trained and committed manpower at all levels. But, the corporate systems are found not to be relevant to this plant. On the other hand, PMS was made applicable to this plant, with effect from 1st April 2000 for all categories with the clear aim to help the staff in improving their performance on the job. PMS provided for developing a nurturing environment of work and so 'coaching' was regarded as the most suitable leadership style that could be applicable in the organisation.

A. K. Chopra took over as CEO of E-mail Engineering Company in mid-2000. He believed in hard work, determination and most of all, honesty in all the work that was done in the organisation. The managers regard the CEO as one who has a road-roller approach to work. The CEO does not falter in using classical techniques of firing, control and strict discipline. He loathes using a softer approach towards industrial relations.

On 1st January 2001, the employees of 'B' shift (2 p.m. to 10 p.m.) staged a drama against a new system of punching attendance through clocks. There was also a general conflict to change over to the new system amid all the employee groups.

The CEO called a meeting of the employees' trade union representatives and explained his grief over the protest caused by the employees. The meeting was inconclusive.

On 3rd January 2001, the management started using disciplinary action against the employees who were protesting in the plant; the employees were suspended until enquiry was done and were served with charge sheets. Further, on 5th January 2001, a group of some ten employees were found to be waiting in the office premises of the plant. The plant office closed as a precaution against further rise in agitation as per the intelligence report of the local government. The local government advised the plant management not to take any action. In view of that, the firm's headquarters was posted with these developments from time to time. The corporate management was apprehensive of awkward situations that may come up in the wake of the whole episode and thus, as a precaution advised the local management not to rush the matter.

By the evening of 6th January 2001, the management was forced to remove the chargesheet that was issued to the employees on the advice of the corporate office.

On 7th January 2001, a conciliatory meeting occurred between the plant management and the employees' representatives. The management decided to resolve all the employees grievances through mutual negotiation and employees representatives agreed to accept the proposals of the management. These proposals included new ways to improve the everyday functioning of the plant. In truth, the management asked the support and participation of each employee in the new schemes in the interest of the plant. The plant then operated peacefully with effect from 8th January 2001.

The performance management system suffered a setback because of the near strike situation caused by the agitational approach of the employees during the month of January 2001.

The CEO of the E-mail Engineering Company had a habit of attacking the managers. On 20th March 2001, the CEO had called a meeting of the senior managers and deputy general managers for a monthly production review. Dejected with the performance of the head of machining section, the CEO got hold of him by his collar and pushed him aside. Incidents of this nature became a custom in the plant, which had a negative effect on the work environment. Managers were unwilling to commit to their work and this was the major causality. By the behaviour of the CEO, the E-mail Engineering Company became a hamstrung organisation. The CEO's behaviour became a barrier for the managers' performance.

The original idea with which performance management was started in the plant, namely, for creation of a nurturing climate for allowing the staff to develop their performance and take care of their personal development was turned into a distant cry, by the end of 2001. Open work environment took a sharp turn for the worst. As such, the work culture became an obstacle for implementing the performance management system (PMS).

By April 2002, PMS turned into a confidential performance appraisal. Subordinates were held responsible for not meeting their targets which were laid down unilaterally by the head of department (HOD). The process of target setting, an agreement on competencies, giving feedback, coaching and counselling plus individual/personal development plan, became outmoded. A characteristic bureaucratic work ambience took hold of the plant. E-mail Engineering Company turned into a sick unit and the head office suggested the plant to BFIR (Board for Industrial Reconstruction).

Questions

1. Analyse the PMS used in E-mail Engineering Company.
2. Analyse the dispute between the workers and the management regarding PMS.

Case 3: Case Study on Performance Management System

The following case study explains how a big firm incorporates the use of values into its performance management system. The case study also explains how the performance management system is successfully used to recognise and develop potential leaders in preparing for a successful planning.

Boral Limited is Australia's biggest building and construction materials supplier. They operate in Australia, the USA and have over 14,700 employees working across 717 functional sites. Boral includes seven important operating divisions, lined up along three business sections. Its aim is to be a value-driven and market-driven building and construction material supplier operating in Australia and gradually more abroad; its overriding goals are to attain great returns in a sustainable way in a financial, social and environmental sense.

The performance management system has basically three steps – first, establishing objectives; second, recognising values and career development; and third, managing performance. Values are used to direct both corporate and personal across all levels of the organisation. The values of leadership, respect, focus, performance and persistence are supported by a complete performance management system which guarantees employees have work and behaviour goals on the basis of the corporate values. These values are referred to in the firm's strategic aim to support their importance in Boral, and are integrated into each employee's annual performance review to evaluate the behaviour of workplace style and effectiveness. Examples of expected behaviour are provided for managers to guarantee a common understanding of Boral's values across the organisation. The values that are shown by the employees are questioned twice annually using the performance management system, and, along with meeting goals, can have an effect on employee pay increases.

These values are also propagated through Boral's leadership programs including the Executive Development Program (EDP) designed for senior managers, the upcoming Management Development Program designed for high performing talented leaders, and the Frontline Leadership Development Program. All development programs are designed to recognise, develop and retain potential first, middle and senior managers. Boral has designed new approaches to develop leadership for example, outward bound experience and using learning and development program to deal with significant business issues.

Boral has placed the EDP as an important program targeting candidates marked down as high potential performers. Their strategies that support this reputation include a meticulous selection process, proactive efforts to acquire organisational buy-in, and the proven track record of the program to deliver tangible developments to the business.

Candidates for the program are chosen through 'calls for nominations'. The completion of an employee's estimate of potential and personal invitation, the feedback of managers, an evaluation of the potential of the candidate and their most likely senior in position in the organisation, and their personal commitment are also considered. Acceptance into the program is a positive reflection of both the candidate's contributions so far and the confidence of others in their ability to deliver in the future. For several employees, this is a chance to show what they are able to accomplish when given the chance.

All the EDP development results are meant to change the learning experience into demonstrated leadership behaviours and competencies that reflect the core values and strategic goals. There are two main procedures that are incorporated into the EDP that guarantee participants implementing what they learn of real-life situations; these are the action learning assignments and the inclusion of a Boral-specific case study.

Boral uses succession planning to recognise talent and future leaders. The process involves evaluating employees' estimated potential and assisting them in managing their career development across the organisation. Boral carries out a formal succession planning process that concentrates on managerial and leadership positions frequently. Recognising potential at more senior levels happens every two years. This allows Boral to recognise talent and future leaders and develop their leaders through supporting individual development plans by taking part in Boral's Leadership Development programs and giving opportunities for internal promotion.

The methodical approach Boral takes to planning allows managers and leaders to support Boral's strategic direction and any related change management strategies.

Questions

1. How does the company integrate the use of values into the Performance Management System?
2. What is the process of Performance Management System stated in this case?
3. Analyse the PMS used in this company.

✱✱✱

2.6 Grievance Handling

Case 1: Improving discipline and grievance procedures: an Acas joint working approach to training line managers and supervisors at Patak's

Background: Patak's is famous in UK for its variety of Indian pickles, chutneys, stir-in cooking sauces and curry pastes. It was set up in the 1950s by the father of the present owner, Kirit Pathak; the business has changed itself from a family company operating out of a small North London kitchen into a multi-national company with an approximate value of £50 million. Over the years, having undergone quick growth, the business presently is located in five areas in UK and employs around 750 staff, most of whom are white. Its biggest factory and headquarters are based in Wigan, an area with a low cultural minority population.

The decision to use Acas: Discipline and grievances was one area where it was felt management would gain from practical training. The human resource manager decided to tackle this problem and asked Acas to help. The main purpose behind the training was to guarantee that all line managers were regular in accepting the best practice by restoring them on the right disciplinary process. Past experience had shown that managers were unsure of their role in enforcing disciplinary matters; they lacked the confidence to handle discipline and grievance situations in a suitable way. Furthermore, they were not always clear about the difference between their role and the role of HR in handling such situations; in some cases, they were too eager to pass discipline and grievance cases straight to HR. Thus the desired result of the training was to give power to managers in this facet of their role by providing them with the required information and skills.

Managers realised that it was significant to get an autonomous third party to run the training on discipline and grievance. The group HR manager at Patak's by now knew the services that Acas gave and had attended network meetings hosted by Acas on employment issues. She felt Acas' neutral approach to employment associations made them perfect to carry out this training on their behalf. Furthermore, Acas was an organisation that was well-known to the employees and this would help to describe the training in a positive rather than a negative light.

What Acas did: Acas consultants decided on a training programme with Patak's that was based around the firm's current policy and procedures on discipline and grievances. The training took the form of half-day workshops which line managers and supervisors were invited to attend. A trade union representative who was a shop floor steward also participated as did a member of HR. Acas ran three of these workshops, with up to 12 delegates in each session. Senior managers at Patak's identified the advantages of accepting a joint working process which involves management and union representatives working together. The belief behind Acas joint working is to motivate individuals from all levels of an organisation to discover and understand problems from different viewpoints.

The workshops covered the following key areas:

- The reasons for discipline: Why it is a need and how it can be seen as a positive way of establishing standards and expectations within an organisation;

- Best practice: The right processes to follow when dealing with discipline and grievance situations;

- Delegate work using real life situations from organisations in the same divisions: Role play exercises gave managers an opportunity to put into practice what they had studied;

- Guidance on dealing with difficult situations: The need to view situations from an objective viewpoint and handle it accordingly, while avoiding conflict and personality clashes.

Managers reported feeling more positive and confident about their capability to handle discipline and grievance circumstances following the workshops. It was felt that Acas had created a climate in which the employees felt comfortable in talking about difficult issues. The combination of methods that the Acas advisers used also helped in making it a productive and pleasant process.

Outcomes of Acas' involvement: As a result of undertaking the training, Acas was capable of giving suggestions to HR staff about making small changes to their policy on discipline and grievances so as to guarantee that it matched the best practice and resolve areas that are open to misunderstanding. Once the HR recommended the changes, they consulted the trade union for their opinion and the segment on discipline and grievances in the employee handbook was modified accordingly.

In the period since the training, absenteeism has gone down and the HR manager felt that more improvements in confidence had happened. Though this is not directly credited to the training, it was felt that the training was among other factors that have helped in contributing to a steadier staff.

Questions

1. How did ACAS find a solution to the grievance that occurred in the company?
2. What was the outcome of Acas' involvement?

Case 2: Case Study on Grievance

The appellant is a nationalised bank and two of the respondents are its employees. The other two are the trade unions that represent the Bank's employees, in continuance of particular demands for wage revision made by the employees in June 1977. All the Indian Bank employees' association called out for an all-India strike on specific days. The bank issued a circular dated 23rd September 1977 to its managers and agents directing them to deduct the salaries of such employees who took part in the strike on the principle of 'no work, no pay'. There was a 4-hour strike on 29th December 1977. The bank issued an administrative circular dated 29th December 1977 to its managers and agents that such employees who took part in the 4-hour strike would be violating their contract of service and would not draw salary for the whole day.

The employees struck work for 4 hours on 29th December 1977. On 16th January 1978 the bank issued a circular to its managers and agents directing them to deduct the full day's income of such employees who had taken part in the 4-hour strike. The respondents filed a writ petition for withdrawing that circular. The petition was allowed. Hence the present appeal was made by the bank.

Questions

1. Was it permissible for the bank, by means of the impugned administrative circular, to deduct a full day's wages (or even a part thereof) of the employees who participated in the 4-hour strike on 29th December 1977?

2. Given that strikes are recognised as a legitimate form of protest for workers, do you think that the bank is justified in suppressing such a legitimate mode of protest by an administrative circular?

3. Which sections of the Payment of Wages Act, 1936 are relevant in this case?

***

Case 3: Protest over Job Losses

Bitter it may taste, shrill it may sound, and sleepless nights it may cause, but it is true. In a major shake-up, Airbus, the European aircraft manufacturer, has thrown a big shock to its employees. Before coming to the details of the shock, a peep into the firm's resume.

Name	:	Airbus
Created	:	1970
President, CEO	:	Louis Gallois
Employees	:	57,000
Turnover (2006)	:	26 billion (Euros)
Total aircraft sold (February 2007)	:	7,187
Delivered	:	4598
Headquarters	:	Toulouse (France)
Facilities	:	16
Rival	:	Boeing

On February 27th 2007 Airbus declared, that it would get rid of 10,000 jobs across four European countries and sell six of its units. On the same day, the unfortunate employees did what was expected of them. They staged protests. The protesting employees at Airbus' factory at Meaulte, Northern France, were seen protesting outside the factory gate after stopping production a day earlier. To be fair to Airbus, its management entered into negotiations with unions before the job loss and the sale was formally declared. But the negotiations did not appease the agitated employees.

Job shedding and employing of units are a part of Power8 reorganisation plan unleashed by Airbus to save itself from increasing loss of its position to the adversary, Boeing Co.

Airbus' Power8 strategy was first suggested in October 2006, but ignited a split between France and Germany over the distribution of job losses, and the placement of future ones. Later on, the two countries decided to share both job losses and new technology.

The Power8 plan, if finalised, would mean a 9 percent decrease in Airbus' 55,000 employee strength.

Questions

1. Why should Power8 focus on shedding jobs to save on cost? Are there no alternative strategies?
2. Will the proposed shedding of jobs and sale of six units help Airbus survive the intense competition from Boeing?

Case 4: A Case on Grievance

Laxmi Brass Products, a Hyderabad-based factory, specialises in the production of types of brass and copper vessels. These vessels were generally used for domestic reasons plus in industries. The factory was founded in 1960 with 75 workmen. Towards the end of 1980s, there were about 800 employees working in the factory.

With the beginning of quick changes in technology as also their consumers' choice, the firm, in agreement with the changing times is now manufacturing copper-base vessels that are needed by modern housewives. They had also introduced copper storage vessels for drinking water in different sizes that ranged from three litres to forty litres.

The factory had certified standing orders under the Industrial Employment Act, 1946. Till 1984, there was no union.

The factory was managed by a general manager, who, consecutively, was helped by a production manager and personnel officer. For any grievance redressal, the employees were required to go to the personnel officer to resolve it to their liking. It was rare that any case was referred to the general manager or the managing director.

Towards the end of 1985, a workman named Santosh Jadhav was found sleeping during the night shift at his workplace near the polishing machine. He was caught in the act by the shift in-charge who was on his rounds at the shop floor. He was woken up by the security guard who was on duty. After being woken, Santosh admitted his fault and requested the management not to take any action.

Next day, he was called to the manager's office and was asked to give his statement in writing. Accordingly, his statement with a request for mercy was documented. On the other hand, as sleeping on duty was a serious misconduct, the workman was released from the services.

Santosh had an authentic reason for having slept on duty on that time; he had to attend to his sick wife and children on the previous night. He was supporting a big family of three children and old parents. He did not put up his defence hoping that he might be discharged, if he admitted his fault.

The dismissal came as a major blow to Santosh and after recovering from this shock, he went to the newly elected union president Ravi Nayar. The latter listened to Santosh understandingly and promised to help him through the union. The union decided to give a monthly amount of Rs. 500 to Santosh as financial help. This incident motivated many employees to volunteer and extend help to Santosh. This helped the union to register about 300 workmen as union members. Santosh found that for the first time in his life he was capable of collecting adequate amount of money as donations and payments from the workmen.

In due course of time, he found the union job more attractive and paying. He liked this job even more than his earlier job. Santosh developed the necessary skills of public speaking, key information about the rights of union and became a union leader. In an efficient way, he listed and recorded many grievances of the workmen. During his communication with other employees, he talked about the living style and condition of workmen – that they were undernourished, ill clothed, without good housing; while the managers had luxurious cars, big bungalows to stay, wore the finest suits, and enjoyed variety of food. He encouraged employees saying that all these comforts enjoyed by the management were given as a result of the efforts of the workmen. Nevertheless, the fruits of their efforts were never shared with them. With such lectures, the union in the factory gained a membership of 90 percent.

Santosh became the general secretary of the union. The union raised many issues on the basis of a list prepared by Santosh such as, wage disputes, payment of bonus, festival holidays, and individual cases of discharge of workmen before the conciliation officer. Some were settled and the remaining cases were referred to the tribunal for settlement. At this phase, the union was not recognised by the management, though they sat with the union before the conciliation officer and tried to finalise the settlements.

The conciliation officer saw that there was no industrial relations committee in the factory, nor was there a forum for an addresser of grievances of the workmen. The conciliation officer insisted that if such a forum was not formed, he would begin proceedings of prosecution against the said factory. The management, though reluctantly, followed the Industrial Disputes Act and called for nominations from the workmen in the formation of Industrial Relations Committee. Despite many efforts, no nominations were received from the workmen and, thus, the management expressed its incapability to create such a committee. No action was initiated by the conciliation officer after receiving these details.

Later, differences in the union came up during the election of the union members regarding the spending of the money which was collected from the members as donations and fees which were utilised towards the election costs. The union also signed a bonus settlement in October, 1985, for bonus at the rate of 8.33 percent for the last financial year, although the factory made good profits in the previous financial year. Incidentally, there were common rumours that Ravi Nayar, the president of the union was paid a sum of ₹ 400,000 to consent to the bonus settlement that was previously described. Santosh was not happy about this, and decided to create a new union with the help of his supporters.

On behalf of the newly formed union, Santosh applied for registration, but the Registrar objected on the issue of dual membership and as the previous union approached and told about this.

Santosh, nevertheless, kept on working under the union. He refused the bonus settlement signed by the previous union under the leadership of Nayar. In the next week, a fresh demand of bonus at the rate of 20 percent was submitted to the management. Together with these, extra demands like increase in dearness allowance, house rate allowance and housing loans were also put in. The new union also aggravated the management by issuing threats that if their demands were not accepted, the workmen would go on strike with effect from 10th December, 1985. A copy of the demands of the union and the notice of the strike was also given so that both parties could negotiate before going to the conciliation officer.

He also proposed that since the union was not yet registered or recognised, it would be wrong for the representative of the employees to represent in the said gathering.

The management absolutely refused to have any talks with the new union and also clearly told all the workmen concerned that the previous bonus settlement still stands, and they were not ready to go through with further talks. Santosh again requested the conciliation officer to interfere but the conciliation officer refused to oblige. After this incident, Santosh threatened to go on strike.

One of Santosh's close aides, Nihal Singh, called a meeting of the workmen in his department and told the workmen that since the management was paying them only 6 percent bonus; while the officers were getting almost 50 percent amount as a performance award every year, they were not doing justice to the employees. The personnel officer called Nihal Singh to his office and told him, "that he should not do such things which might worsen the situation". But he did not listen to him and again joined the crowd.

Later, someone from the mob shouted – *Mar Dalo! Kill them!* following which the crowd threateningly rushed towards the cabin of the personnel manager. The personnel manager was surrounded by the employees and they began to beat him. Nonetheless, Nihal Singh interfered and managed to save the personnel officer before the crowd went wild.

The personnel manager lost his consciousness; he was moved to a hospital, and, afterwards, was released. On 10th December, the employees went on strike as per their notice.

Questions

1. What is the real problem in the case?

2. As an HR manager, how would you have handled the situation in the above case? What proactive actions would you take to avoid the present situation?

3. Do you justify the dismissal of Santosh Jadhav?

4. Give a suitable title for the above case.

***

2.7 Settlement of Industrial Disputes – Industrial Relations

Case 1: State Road Transport Corporation

A State Road Transport Corporation has been giving passenger transportation facilities since 1966. It has been extending its operations from one area to another by nationalising the private passenger transport firms in stages. Currently, it is operating its services in 80 percent of the routes in the State. It nationalised two routes in East Godavari District in the State in October, 1999. Generally, it attracts all the employees working in passenger transport firms before getting nationalised and sets their incomes equally with the scales of similar groups of jobs in the company.

The pay scale in the corporation is determined based on mutual agreement between the management and the trade union that is recognised. The scales are changed once in three years and the current agreement came into force with effect from September, 1999. There are two groups in the driver category, that is, Class I drivers (working on long distance buses) and Class II drivers (working on short distance routes). The salaries of Class II drivers is improved from ₹ 2,800-4,200 to ₹ 4,000-6,000 (with effect from September, 1999) as a result of the latest agreement. The agreement further says that the salaries of the drivers drawing pay in the scale of ₹ 2,800-4,200 will be set in the scale of ₹ 4,000-6,000.

The company hired 10 drivers who were with the private passenger transport firms resulting on the recent nationalisation of two routes. The employees department fixed the scale of these 10 drivers in the scale of ₹ 2,800-4,200 and it declined their pleas of fixing their pay in the scale of ₹ 4,000-6,000 saying that only the drivers drawing the scale of ₹ 4,000-6,000 are now qualified to draw the new scale of ₹ 4,000-6,000. The company has established both the grievance machinery and the collective bargaining machinery to resolve employee issues. These drivers submitted this issue to the foreman who is their direct superior. The foreman told them to raise this issue in collective bargaining with the assistance of trade union leaders as it is a policy. These drivers approached the trade union leaders and convinced them to take up the issue. The trade union included this item in the draft agenda of the approaching meeting of the collective bargaining committee. But the collective bargaining committee removed this item from the draft agenda saying that this issue can be settled though grievance machinery as only 10 drivers out of 3,000 drivers of the corporation are concerned with this matter.

Questions

1. Among the personnel department, the foreman, and the collective bargaining committee, who is correct?

2. Where is this issue to be placed for redressal?

3. How would you redress this grievance?

***

Case 2: Case Study on Industrial Dispute

This case is based on a petition filed by a workman under Articles 226 and 227 of the constitution against the disputed award passed by the labour court, Amritsar answering the reference for the respondent-management. The case of the management lies in the testimony of its own witness (MW-1). The petitioner was selected and joined duty at the Government College for Women, Amritsar on 25th September 1991. On 9th May 1992, the head girl to the principal reported misbehaviour of the petitioner, in which the petitioner was discharged from the services or 14th May 1992. The foundation of the order lay in misconduct; no charge sheet was issued to her, nor was any basic enquiry held to establish the misconduct before such termination. No chance was given to the employee to counter the report of the head girl and the mess president, or to meet the complainant with a defence at cross-examination. There was no prior warning letter issued by the management leading to the action taken on 9th May 1992. As a result, the petitioner served the college from 25th September 1991 to 14th May 1992, that is, for 233 days.

The MW-1 confessed that the job was permanent in nature and the employee's services were terminated for misconduct. The defence of the management before the labour court was that the employee had put in only 233 days of service and thus she had obtained no industrial rights; she was removed from service in terms of her appointment letter under which her service could be terminated at any time, without any notice.

The appointment was a regular one and not contractual. It may have been temporary employment not shortened by time, but the management could not have so simply proposed the clause in the appointment letter allowing it to discharge the employee from service at any time, without any prior notice. The labour court just closed the door for the petitioner on the ground that 240 days service had not been put in. It further failed to address itself to the core question that putting in of 240 days of nonstop service does not come up in case of misconduct.

Afterwards, the court permitted the writ petition and invalidated the disputed award. The petitioner was directed to be reinstated with continuity of service and full back-wages. On the other hand, the management was given the freedom to hold fresh enquiry on the same allegations according to the law but only after implementing the court's order.

Questions

1. Do you think that the respondent-management was right in abruptly terminating the services of the petitioner 7 days short of completing 240 days on the ground of misconduct? What were the lacunae on the part of the management in the case?

2. Would termination of services of the petitioner in an admitted case of misconduct, 7 days short of completing 240 days amount to unfair labour practice? Argue with logic.

3. Was the decision of the labour court fair? Justify.

4. Which sections of the Industrial Disputes Act, 1947 are relevant in this case?

Case 3: An Interstate or NSW Dispute?

In 1928 coal miners in the Hunter Valley of NSW declined a proposal put by the employers and the state government that a decrease in the price of coal should be accompanied by an equal decrease in their wages. The employers replied by closing the mines and 'locking out' the miners from their place of work until they agreed to the wage cut. This work strike lasted for 16 months and 10,000 workers were removed. The NSW government then interfered with the ultimatum that if the miners did not accept the 1928 plan the government would reopen the mines, paying the decreased wage rates. This threat of forcibly reopening the mines by government action caused unrest in the coal mines in Queensland and Victoria, as the miners at these places dreaded the cut in wages in NSW would ultimately result in decrease in their own wages. In late 1928 one of the NSW mines was reopened by the NSW government. The miners' union notified the (then) Commonwealth Court of Conciliation and Arbitration of the existence of an interstate industrial dispute. The arbitration court found that either an industrial dispute was present or one was 'threatened and impending', and therefore had jurisdiction to resolve the dispute. On the other hand, on appeal to the High Court of Australia, it was believed that no interstate industrial dispute existed, as the dispute was confined to NSW alone.

Questions

1. Discuss the reasons for concluding that this was an interstate dispute.
2. Discuss the reasons for concluding that the dispute was confined to NSW.

✶✶✶

Case 4: The Hunter Valley Dispute

The decision of the AIRC in the Hunter Valley mine dispute has been held by some observers as a watershed moment in the history of the federal tribunal, in that it marked the end of its influence in Australian industrial relations. The controversial decision came in October 1999 after a quarrel involving 16 weeks of friction and several litigations between one of the world's biggest mining firms, Rio Tinto, and the mining division of the Construction, Forestry, Mining and Energy Union (CMFEU). The decision was significant because it was viewed as a test of the bargaining provisions that were revised in the Workplace Relations Act 1996, which more closely interprets the commission's role as arbitrator in prolonged company bargaining disputes.

The origins of the dispute go back to 19th December 1995, when representatives of the CFMEU met with the management of the Hunter Valley No. 1 mine to begin company negotiations for a certified agreement. On the other hand, industrial strain between the parties soared in the coming months as negotiations slowed and the

CFMEU got involved in industrial action in reply to the direct and quick dismissal of a mine site truck driver. In addition, negotiations were made more complex by the size and importance of management's claim and the union opposition to agree to the demands. Management had sought substantial changes to work rules including the elimination of seniority which had conventionally been the basis for promotion and retention and a decrease in union control at the place of work. As Michael Angevin (then chief employee relations advisor for Rio Tinto) explained:

"Australian coal producers including ourselves need to be more competitive so that we know from the benchmarking work about what we've done and that others have done, the reasons why we're uncompetitive, relative to those new competitors. It's mostly because of poor work practices, which have been a legacy of the earlier economic content when management leadership was underdeveloped and all the variety of systems under which our employees work were based outside the company. They were based on the activities of unions and not ourselves. Faced with that economic context a business like ours doesn't have much choice except to develop its work practices, improve the human resource systems under which our employees work" (**Waring 2000**).

By March of 1997, the important elements of the Workplace Relations Act 1996 had come into effect, including Australian Workplace Agreements (AWAs) – statutory individual contracts. Some observers have advised that, for Rio Tinto management, the Act provided new opportunities to execute individualised employment relations and increase managerial caution at the Hunter Valley mine. Using individualised employment relations to lessen the power of the union and increase managerial privilege was a strategy that Rio Tinto had accepted at several other operations around the world with some success. It is also a strategy that it had adopted at its bauxite operations in Weipa in Queensland, which resulted in a national dispute in 1995.

CFMEU officials said that the wages and conditions that were improved were tied to the acceptance of the AWAs, but that the strategy was nothing like that at Weipa. As Tony Maher (CFMEU national president) explained:

"If you look at the bargaining strategy in the Hunter Valley mine dispute, the bargaining strategy of the company was sort of a 'reverse Weipa hold'. It wasn't the Weipa hold, it was, 'here's what we'll offer as an individual contract. And if you want a collective agreement we'll offer less, and if you knock that back we'll offer less again' (**Waring 2000**).

Finally, only a small number of miners accepted the AWAs, but the strategy put a lot of pressure on the union under to agree to the management's demands. The union's counter-strategy at the height of the dispute was to call on the AIRC to end the bargaining period and settle the dispute. The firm on the other hand, refused the calls to settle the dispute. The general manger, Alan Davies, insisted that a third party solution was no solution to the mine's challenges.

"I guess what was different about it was that it was one of the first disputes in the coat industry which occurred under the new WRA 1996 where, automatically because there was a dispute the Commission wasn't asked to step in and make some decision which it knew nothing about and nothing about the business" **(Waring 2000).**

Rio Tinto answered the calls to finish the bargaining period by sending all striking miners a copy of a posed, non-union, certified agreement. They also effectively sought through Section 135 of the Workplace Relations Act 1996, a secret ballot of all striking miners, in an effort to finish the dispute. In the introduction to the ballot, Alan Davies appeared in numerous television advertisements and placed advertisements in local print media urging miners to vote yes to end the nine-week-long strike.

On Friday 7th November 1997, the Hon. Justice Boulton of the AIRC agreed with the submissions of the FMEU, the Australian Council of Trade Unions and the South Wales government that he should pass judgement to resolve 'this battle of the titans'.

Rio Tinto replied to the Hon. Justice Boulton's decision to end the bargaining periods at the Hunter Valley mine by successfully requesting the original decision. A full bench of the AIRC overturned the previous decision by the Flora, Justice Boulton to end the bargaining periods at the Hunter Valley mine and to arbitrate. The president of the AIRC, the Hon. Justice Giudice, concluded that 'it was unreasonable for Boulton J. to have been pleased that industrial action being taken was threatening to cause danger to the welfare of the people of the Hunter Valley, which had been the legal trigger for the Hon, Justice Boulton to appeal to the AIRC in the disputes. Later, Mick Kelly (CFMEU official) would remark:

"The decision gave an upper hand to the firm. It permitted them to continue with the decrease in bonus, abolition of tolerance time, decrease in shift penalties – it basically authorised them to do what they wanted."

Following its successful plea, Rio Tinto carried out its secret ballot in mid May 1998 with the help of the Australian Electoral Commission (AEC). Of the 372 CFMEU and

Australian Manufacturing Workers Union members at the mine, only 28 voted for Rio Tinto's proposed agreement. Following the ballot, in October 1998, the firm through a round of forced retrenchments, decreased the Hunter Valley workforce by about 115 employees. Afterwards, these retrenchments were the topic of a successful unfair dismissal claim that brought about a multi-million dollar settlement in 1998. The CFMEU pleaded against the full bench of the AIRC's decision not to arbitrate and the full bench of the Federal Court of Australia issued a decision that successfully overturned the earlier decision and order and refused to interfere in the dispute. The decision effectively needed the full bench of the AIRC to re-hear the matter along with the principles decided by the Federal Court.

The result of the ballot, combined with a new decision from the full bench of the AIRC in May 1999, declaring that they would now arbitrate the dispute, revived the hopes of the CFMEU officials and delegates. Their optimism was on the basis of the firm's actions and the mine's own 88.5 million profit in the 1998 to 1999 period, which was an amazing result in the context of historically low coal prices. Given this, the union leaders considered that the ARC would grant wages and conditions comparable to market rates or no less than what those who had accepted the AWAs were getting.

These hopes were ruined in October 1999 when a full bench of the Commission handed down its arbitrated award. In a decision that was highly controversial, the AIRC declined the CFMEUs claims that it should arbitrate an award that is the same as the benefits to industry certified agreements and, instead, decided that the coal industry award and a slightly improved coal bonus should belong to the mine.

For the firm, the decision was a turning point. It had been capable of securing all kinds of flexibilities besides lowering take-home pay, and it had successfully received the AIRC approval for doing so. In actual fact, the full bench often used the word 'all's fair in love and war' in their decision to state their reluctance to change the result of what they described as 'industrial warfare'. The decision has been claimed by some to mark the end of the federal tribunal because although the AIRC had been forced to interfere in the dispute, it had declined to meddle with the status quo, the result of the industrial conflict between the parties.

Questions

1. If you were the member of the tribunal allocated the Hunter Valley No. 1 mine dispute, how would you have tried to help them resolve their differences?

2. Should the tribunals be allowed to intervene and arbitrate in disputes such as the Hunter Valley No. 1 mine dispute?

3. Does anyone win in long-running disputes, like the Hunter Valley mine dispute, where the parties are continuously in and out of the tribunals and the courts?

***

Case 5: Toyota Strike Case

Toyota manufactures world famous cars like Corolla, Camry and Innova at its plant. Toyota Kirloskar Motor Private Limited was established as a joint venture in 1997, between Japan's biggest car firm and the world's second-biggest car manufacturer – Toyota Motor Corporation (Toyota) and the Kirloskar Group of India. The plant had a total workforce of 2,378, of which around 1,550 employees belonged to the employees' union. Toyota holds an 89 percent equity stake while the Kirloskar Group holds the remaining 11 percent. Toyota has invested nearly US $336 million in the factory with an ability to produce 60,000 units per year.

On 8th January, 2006, Toyota Kirloskar Motor Private Limited (TKM) declared an indefinite lock-out of its vehicle manufacturing plant at Bidadi located near Bangalore, Karnataka. The decision was taken following a strike, which had entered its third day, by the Toyota Kirloskar Motor Employees Union, the only recognised union. The lock-out notice stated that the strike was unlawful as the employees' union did not give a compulsory fourteen-day notice period as per Industrial Disputes Act, 1947.

It also stated that the employees were behaving violently. On January 6, 2006, the employees' union went on strike with the following demands, namely, the reinstatement of three dismissed employees; cancel the suspension orders of ten suspended employees, for bringing about improved working conditions at the factory.

The employees were dismissed and suspended by the firm, for attacking a supervisor, indulging in misconduct, respectively. Toyota Kirloskar Motor declared that it would neither re-employ nor reinstate those employees – this declaration concluded in a strike and lock-out. Toyota Kirloskar Motor made many serious allegations against the employees' union. The firm said that the striking workers were threatening to blow up LPG gas cylinders in the company premises, obstructing the outward movement of manufactured vehicles, unlawfully stopping production, and manhandling other workers, who were not part of the employees' union.

In response, the employees' union said that three employees were dismissed because they were actively taking part in trade union activities and the firm wanted to suppress the trade union. They further said that working conditions at the factory were inhuman and slave-like.

They were frequently made to stretch their working hours without enough relaxation and compensation. The issue took a serious turn when representatives from the management at Toyota Kirloskar Motor declined to attend a meeting before the Labour Commissioner on January 9th, 2006, for resolving the dispute with the union.

The firm said that the atmosphere was not conductive for talks as the employees' union was in a violent and agitated mood. Though, the firm appealed for two weeks time to appear before the Labour Commissioner so that situation could become steady, they were given time only till 12th January, 2006.

The employees' union got support from different trade unions and demanded the involvement of the state government to assist in resolving the dispute in their favour.

Toyota Kirloskar Motor continued to partially produce vehicles with the help of non-unionised workers and the management staff. The latter were specially trained for these kinds of emergencies. On the other hand, the company's output had fallen from 92 vehicles per day to 30 vehicles with an estimated production loss of around 700 million rupees.

The company lifted the lockout on 21st January, 2006, stating that it was responding to the request from workers who were ready to return to work. The workers were required to sign a good conduct undertaking to maintain discipline and guarantee full production.

The Employees' Union gave in and withdrew their strike following a government order on 21st January, 2006, which was against the strike and referred the issue to the third additional labour court. On the other hand, the union said that they would not sign the good conduct declaration specified by Toyota Kirloskar Motor Private Limited.

The unrest had other consequences as the Toyota spokesperson said that the company would reconsider its recent decision to build a second car manufacturing factory in the state.

It was also felt that this incident would seriously have an effect on the Government of Karnataka's efforts insofar as persuading Volkswagen to set up a vehicle manufacturing plant in the state. This was the second dispute involving a Japanese vehicle manufacturer and trade unions in India. This latest rise in trade union activism resulting in violence and business loss has attracted the attention of the national and international media.

Questions

1. What was the main cause of lock-out as per the Toyota Kirloskar management?

2. According to you, was the union the real cause of strike?

3. If you are the personnel manager in the situation, what different options would you propose to the management? Justify your proposals.

4. Give your views on engaging non-unionised employees for production during strikes.

Case 6: A Case on Noble Paper Industry

Noble Paper Industry is situated in a backward zone of Raigad district. It employs about six hundred employees. The firm was founded in 1988. Throughout the first six years from its foundation, it did neither make any profits and nor did it pay any statutory bonus. But to sustain with other neighbouring firms, this firm paid an ex-gratia payment once every year to its employees at a flat rate of ₹ 2,000 per employee. The firm began to pay statutory bonus since the payment of Bonus Act become applicable. Additionally, the firm decided to stop the practice of ex-gratia payment. Employees, through the trade union, started protesting.

After an extensive round of discussions when the union realised that the management was determined on not giving ex-gratia it suddenly, announced a strike. Officers were threatened and the employees behaved with them violently. Production had completely stopped. The firm suffered heavy losses. The Management approached Labour Court and requested to declare strike as illegal. The Court declared the strike as illegal since 14 days' notice was not given.

Some attempts were made by the local leaders to resolve the dispute, but the management was not agreeable now. The Management decided to remove the recognition that was accorded to the Union, as per the provisions under the related law. As a result of this step, the doors of negotiations and compromise between Management and Union were permanently closed. Further, the deadlock has deteriorated as some of the office bearers of the Union have threatened the Management of terrible consequences, unless they fulfil the Union's demand instantly.

Questions

1. Comment on the role played by the Union in insisting on exgratia payment in addition to bonus.
2. Evaluate the Union's action of declaring sudden strike especially when the Management was willing to negotiate with it.
3. Is the step of de-recognising Union by the Management appropriate as seen from the angle of maintaining smooth industrial relations? Explain in detail the reasons for proper or improper decision of the Management.

***

Case 7: A Case on Sweeper Dispute

XYZ Ltd. is a food processing industry. The company employs 22 workers. Earlier the company had in its employment a sweeper, who maintained the cleanliness of the entire company including that of the toilets. This sweeper resigned for personnel reasons and in a hurry, the personnel officer employed a new sweeper.

The new sweeper worked diligently. But the day he was asked to clean the toilets, he refused to do so. He said he was prepared for do any except cleaning of the toilets. In the meanwhile, the workers had joined the XYZ employees union.

The personnel officer called the union leaders for discussion on the problem to resolve the impasse. The union leader contended that the workman was employed as a "sweeper" and not a "wet sweeper". While joining work, he was not told that he would have to clean toilets. He was a diligent worker, but he was not prepared to do demeaning work like cleaning toilets. The management was asked to employ another "wet sweeper" only for cleaning the toilets. The union was threatening to call a strike if there were no settlements of the dispute.

The management contended that hygiene is very important in the food processing industry. The earlier sweeper had done all the work including cleaning toilets. Employing an additional "wet sweeper" was beyond the financial capacity of the company and anyway there was not enough work to be given to him throughout the day.

Questions

1. What do you think of the manner in which the new sweeper was recruited?
2. What do you say about attitude of the union, the new sweeper and the personnel officer in this case?
3. What is the way out to solve impasse?

***

2.8 Transfer, Promotion, and Demotion

Case 1: A Case on Promotion

When Ramesh joined Axis Bank in 1987, he had one clear goal, namely, to prove his potential. He did achieve his goal and had been promoted five times since his joining. Compared to others, his progress was seen as being stellar. Currently, his job entailed working till late hours, and Ramesh worked for almost twelve hours daily and with no holidays. In addition to this, Ramesh was required to travel out of state twice in a month.

His colleagues at the bank appreciated his excellence at work. They held no grudges about his success which had been achieved in a very short span of time. However, some of them believed that they should be promoted as well. Later, due to superannuation, there was a vacancy for the post of senior manager. Ramesh applied for the post along with others in the bank. The deputy general manager told Ramesh that the post would be his.

However, a sudden incident wrecked Ramesh's chances to become the senior manager. The bank had the practice of conducting annual medical checkups of all the staff members. The medical report was directly submitted to the managing director along with measures or precautions to be taken. Though Ramesh was below the age of 40, he too was required to undergo the test.

The managing director received a copy of Ramesh's medical examination results, along with a note from the doctor. In the note, it was mentioned that Ramesh was seriously burdened and stressed and was thus facing high blood pressure problems. The doctor recommended that he needed to be given some rest at least for three weeks. The doctor also recommended that along with taking a break, he needed to exercise and practice yoga. It was also mentioned in the report that if he did not follow this, he would be in danger of having heart problems in another couple of months.

After reading the doctor's note, the managing director thought over the situation and tried to find some solutions to the following questions:

(i)   How would Ramesh take the news?

(ii) How many others would have similar fitness problems?

(iii) As the work system has created the problem, what could the management do to alleviate it?

The idea of holding a stress management programme flashed in his mind, and he immediately summoned his secretary and directed him to hold a meeting with the doctor on a priority basis in this regard for the senior executives.

Questions

1. What could be done to improve the work environment in the above case?
2. Imagine you have to handle the situation. What would you suggest to Ramesh?
3. What could be Ramesh's possible reaction after getting the medical report?

Case 2: Case Study: Possible Demotion of a Long-Time and Faithful Employee

Background: Lucas was a General Clerk I in the general accounting department for eight years and had worked for 28 years with the ABC firm. He was a member of the International Brotherhood of Electrical Workers (IBEW) and was considered a "role model" because he had a perfect attendance work record all through his term with the firm. His main responsibility as a General Clerk I was to make different financial statements and reports for the ABC firm. The General Clerk I was the highest level bargaining unit clerical position in the union contract and the salary was $21.85 per hour.

Just about six months ago, a new department head was selected to the general accounting department. The newly selected department head carried out different audits of the work performance of each employee. He quickly found out that Lucas could not perform the important aspects of his job. After a series of performance meetings with Lucas and extra training by the union, Lucas still could not perform his assigned work projects. Moreover, it was disclosed that other bargaining unit employees had performed Lucas' financial reports for the past eight years. After extensive consultation with the human resource department, it was suggested that Lucas be assessed by the medical department at the ABC firm. After a series of psychological and aptitude tests, it was decided that Lucas had the mental capacity of a fifth grader even though he was forty-five years old. Thus, he could not perform the important aspects of the General Clerk I position.

Union's Position: There were no performance reviews carried out or any written documentation to show that Lucas was not doing his job. It had been the main responsibility of management to tell him that he had not been performing the important aspects of his job in the past eight years. The determination of the new department head was considered by the Union as just a "witch hunt" being conducted by a new department head who desired to be recognised as a "rising star" by the senior leadership at the firm. Therefore, Lucas should not be demoted and salary should not be taken away from him.

Company's Position: This was a very unfortunate condition for both the firm and Lucas. The company granted that Lucas has been a "role model" employee regarding his perfect attendance record for his term at the firm. In simple terms, his record was amazing. On the other hand, the fact remained that Lucas could not do the important duties and responsibilities of the General Clerk I position in the general accounting department. This is an important job position in the general accounting department, particularly in preparing and translating different financial reports that must be performed by the individual serving in this job capacity. This was not a "witch hunt" being conducted by management, but somewhat an attempt to resolve a work performance issue with an employee who did not have the mental capabilities to do his job. Lucas was merely promoted to this clerical position, according to the seniority provision of the collective bargaining agreement between the firm and IBEW. The management took complete responsibility for not conducting proper performance reviews. It is the objective of the management, with extensive consultation with the medical department, to relocate Lucas to a job for which he could perform that job assignment.

Questions

1. Analyse Lucas' case and give a proper solution.
2. Do you think that the company could have stopped Lucas' retrenchment?

Case 3: Old Order Changeth?

Modern Industries Limited (MIL) in Bangalore is an automobile industry. The firm began to manufacture automotive parts twenty years ago in a small way and has gradually developed over the years, employing over 4,000 individuals at present with the turnover exceeding ₹ 100 crores. Its products are selling well and earning a sizable amount of profits.

The firm is managed by an industrialist family known for their shrewdness and business insight. They are among the first generation industrialists who began their industrial enterprises in a modest way, throughout the stage of industrialisation in the country and together with the growth of automotive industry, MIL also expanded.

The current chairman, Suresh Shah, had been with the firm right from its foundation. He started his career as an engineer trainee, rose to the position of the managing director and in 1983 became the firm's chairman. As a result, he is acquainted with every employee who has been in the firm for long. He continues to keep in touch with them and is simply reachable to all of them, overruling hierarchy. A high premium is placed on their loyalty and their long services are appreciated. The chairman of the company strongly believes that each one of them has contributed considerably towards the growth of the firm, considering the fact that the firm maintained a "strong utilitarian culture" all along the contribution of each and every employee had to be significant and they were also rewarded, for that reason. Simultaneously, there were also many instances, where the services were ended because of inadequate performance.

Over twenty years ago, Janardhan Thakur joined MIL as a training instructor. Earlier to that he was an instructor at an industrial training institute. He himself had got the craft instructors' certificate from ITI. He was 35 years old and his chief task was to recruit young individuals as trainees, either under the Apprentices Act or as company employees and then train them as craftsmen. Most of the trainers were absorbed in meeting the growing requirements of the firm, and Shah used to personally engage himself in the process of recruitment and training of craftsmen. Thakur was directly reporting to Shah, in spite of there being a huge gap in the hierarchy. Thakur was promoted to the rank of training superintendent in 1980, though there was much change in his job content. The growing phase of the firm was almost over by that time and the apprentice became just a statutory activity. The firm did not have the vacancies to absorb the trained apprentices, and therefore Shah's involvement in apprenticeship training gradually diminished. The training activity became an additional activity and was not given much value.

The winds of change were blowing through MIL also. Anil Shah, the son of the founder industrialist took over as the managing director of MIL in 1993, whereas Ramesh Shah remained the chairman of the firm.

The young MD was full of new ideas. He wanted to modernise the firm from all facets and expand into high technology areas. He wanted to modernise the current plant and change the management style from the conventional direct control approach to a systems controlled approach. A modern computer was bought and computerisation was introduced.

The firm had to encounter several issues while introducing these changes. One of the major barriers was the problem of some senior employees, who were not qualified or developed, but were promoted to senior positions. Earlier the criterion was loyalty and hard work, rather than competence. Considering this situation, new competent professionals had to be employed to introduce the changes.

MIL was famous for its aggressive personnel policies. Anyone who joined the firm had to put a lot of efforts to survive as the firm was cruel in sacking those who were not meeting the requirements. It was especially so in case of the new appointees, which in turn required them to be merciless in their work. The older employees felt threatened and disliked the changes and the resulting pressures. Thus, they together approached the chairman and requested him to get involved and protect their interests. The chairman, who was not himself satisfied with all the changes, issued instructions to the MD, to the effect that no old employees be displaced. The new MD had no other choice but to abide by the order.

The MD was interested in trying out HRD approaches to train all the employees, mainly those employees who were turning out to be dead wood. He employed Kumar in 1984 as a training manager. Kumar was mainly an engineer but had many years of experience with a multinational firm in the field of HRD, especially in training and management development. He reorganised the training set-up by introducing two assistant managers. Thakur was next to the assistant managers in the hierarchy and reported to Kumar directly and kept on managing the affairs connected to apprenticeship training.

Until Kumar came along, Thakur had benefitted from the position of the head of the training division, though there was no other training division and other training activity excluding apprenticeship training. He was working alone and was reporting directly to the MD. He kept on doing so even after the organisation had grown in proportion. Thakur felt demoted in the new company. He lost his position and individualism in the organisation, and his pride was seriously hurt. He was not prepared to accept Kumar as his boss and he began to behave in an unreasonable manner. He disliked the huge gap created between him and the senior person in the new structure.

Kumar tolerated him hoping that Thakur would settle himself to the changes, in time. Unfortunately he kept on behaving in a similar manner and there was no improvement even after one year. When Kumar tried to counsel him, Thakur demanded to be promoted to the level of assistant manager, as he was the senior most person in the department.

Kumar promised to look into his demand. On a careful analysis of the personal documents of Thakur, he found out that Thakur was over-promoted and also overpaid for the job that he was doing. Leave alone being entitled for further promotion, Thakur was not even fit for his current position.

The company did not have a formal performance appraisal system. Its products were selling well, the profitability was good and therefore all the employees were rewarded well. Promotions and extra increments were given randomly on the basis of the personal likes and dislikes of the senior man, rather than on any objective analysis of performance or potential of a person. No formal manpower planning or organisational planning existed. In future no efforts were made to predict implications of such a system. Overall, the firm did not have any formal projection for the future.

The firm continued the practice of giving long service certificates and awards to all those who had finished 20 years of service in the firm. Thakur had just got his certificates. There were many employees who belonged to Thakur's group. All of them came together and met to talk about their strategies and demands. They used to put up their grievances to the management together. They had established a very strong bond with the chairman, Shah.

Kumar presented all the facts to Thakur to persuade him that his position was not possible. As Thakur was not used to the kind of logic presented by Kumar, he dismissed all his arguments as refined jargon, inappropriate to the context of his firm. He was mostly bitter about the fact that this promotion was turned down whereas there were many people with the same background who have got their promotions. Therefore, there was further deterioration in his behaviour. He began to ignore the directions of Kumar and worked as per his own whims and fancies, behaving proudly. He even went to the point of challenging Kumar that he could neither promote him nor demote him in the current circumstance. So long as he was protected by the chairman of the firm, there was nothing for him to worry about and his job was basically safe.

Kumar hoped that Thakur could conquer his frustration and anger over a period of time. Unfortunately, even after another six months, there was no sign of any development. In reality, the condition worsened further with Thakur becoming more confident in his conviction that Kumar had no power to handle him. He turned out to be a drag in the department, deliberately creating problems for Kumar.

In MIL, the yearly increments and general raises were given as a policy to every employee which was termed as the "janta raise". Thakur was fairly certain that he would get his 'janta raise' and reconciled himself to that Kumar tried to stop his raise but could not do so. There were many bullies who belonged to Thakur's group in the organisation and one of the tasks of the training manager was to deal with such people. Although he had organised a few training workshops in the behavioural areas, it had not brought about the necessary attitudinal changes. Right under his nose he had an individual whose behaviour he was not capable of improving. Kumar realised that the required changes were impossible, so long as the "flat security" was there.

Because of a change in the governmental policy, there were many new competitors to MIL and the MD felt that to make the company more competitive there was a strong need to bring about changes. It was no longer feasible to carry on the organisational dead wood. Kumar was under great pressure to look into all such cases in the organisation, on a priority basis. When he explained his problems, the MD advised him to talk with the chairman about the related facts.

Kumar met the chairman and apprised him of the circumstances mostly citing the example of Thakur. The chairman, in turn accused Kumar himself, questioning him as to why a loyal and normal employee had become problematic under Kumar within one year.

Kumar is now left with no choice but to pay no attention to Thakur and continue in his efforts to change the other difficult employees, though, he will not have the moral right to interfere in such cases. On the other hand, he could simply promote Thakur and buy peace regardless of whether he deserves it or not.

Questions

1. Is it right on the part of the chairman to protect the senior employees, thereby causing problems to the new MD?

2. Is not the chairman over-rewarding long service?

3. Are the senior employees too sensitive and over-reacting to the changes?

4. Did the MD adequately prepare the ground for introducing the changes? Was he too hasty?

5. Would it not have been wise for Kumar to promote Thakur without bothering about the logic which is not applicable in MIL?

6. Is the assumption of the training manager that 'over-protection is the root cause of trouble' right?

Case 4: A Case on Internal Promotion

RK Fabricators, a medium-sized company was engaged in the fabrication of heavy structures. The company was spread over at six different locations. Each location was managed independently for engineering activities and administrative activities like Finance, Human Resource, Marketing etc. and were separately managed centrally by the head office. It employed over 5,000 people. The chief executive officer was the overall in-charge for the activities of the entire company.

In one of the plants, about 900 employees were working, and they provided the heavy fabricated structure for machine tools, structure for automated conveyors used in large plants for manufacturing of automobiles, auto components suppliers etc. The day-to-day management was carried out through a plant manager who was assisted by a couple of engineers and supervisors. There are three main departments in the plant; they were cutting, welding and assembly. In the cutting and welding department, the work was supervised by two engineers who, were, in turn, assisted by three supervisors in each section. The cutting section was directly under the supervision of one of the engineers and they got their information directly from the planning department about the size of the material to be cut as per the orders. The priority of the work was set by the engineer and supervisors as per urgency. The section had about 100 workmen on its rolls.

In 2001, the shop started receiving heavy orders and the workload also increased considerably. The engineer and the two supervisors were unable to cope up with it. On the plant manager's recommendations, the CEO sanctioned two posts of supervisors for the cutting section. As there was a shortage of a supervisor in the welding departments, one supervisor was transferred to the welding department. Now, there was shortage of one supervisor in the cutting section. One of the fitters, Nitin Patil, who had completed his NCTVT examination along with ITI, had been working in the company for the last six years. He was educated in an English medium school and was good in both speaking and writing in English.

The engineer who was working in the cutting section knew Patil very well, so he recommended Patil's name for the post of the supervisor in the same section. As per the company's norms, the minimum qualification for supervisor should be diploma in mechanical engineering. The HR department had given the advertisement for the same, but they could not get a suitable person for the post.

Nitin Patil was also the general secretary of the union. As per the practice, all the union members were also working along with other workmen on the shop floor. Patil being a secretary of the union was very sincere in his work. And because of his position and knowledge, he was respected in his department by his co-workers.

The manager of the plant forwarded Patil's recommendation to the plant manager who, in turn, discussed this with the CEO. The CEO did not agree for two reasons –

(a) He is already a general secretary of the union, so he should resign from the post first, and

(b) His qualifications were not as per the requirements of the post.

These points were communicated to Patil as well as the engineer in the cutting department. After getting this reply, the union president and general secretary met the CEO.

They discussed the following points with the CEO –

(a) As per the policy of the company, the supervisor is also a member of the union, and

(b) Though Patil had not passed his diploma in engineering, the management could compare his performance at work with any supervisor working in the company and, if Patil did not match the level of performance with them, he would withdraw his name from supervisor's post.

After prolonged discussions, the CEO conceded that in the above circumstances, Patil should be given an opportunity to prove himself on the job. It was also agreed that if Patil wished, he should be given guidance for a period of one month by the engineer concerned and, then, could be absorbed subject to the results of a test by the training officer and, in case he passed the said test, he would be promoted as supervisor.

The Union President and Patil accepted the proposal and finally, Patil was promoted as a supervisor after three months.

Questions

1. Analyse the case and identify the main points.

2. If you were the human resource manager in RK Fabricators, what advice would you give to the CEO?

3. Do you agree with the decision taken by the CEO to promote Patil? From an HR viewpoint, what could be the consequences of the decision in future?

***

Case 5: Clerk at Koyali

In May 1985, a vacancy came up in Grade 11-10 of Sr. Clerk at Koyali. At that time the following clerical employees were employed at Koyali.

Sr. No.	Name	Emp. No.	Salary Grade	Date of Joining Grade	Date in present Grade
1.	A. J. Solanki	002165	M-09	26-11-79	04-84
2.	R. B. Diaz	002851	M-09	02-08-82	07-85
3.	R. G. Brah	004408	M-08	21-01-85	01-85
4.	P. M. Pathak	000447	M-08	08-03-85	03-85

For getting promoted to a higher grade in a clerical team, the following norms were considered as per the Promotion Policy Settlement signed with the union in August 1984 which was later altered in May 1986.

1. Seniority determined as per the type and grade of the employees on the basis of marks assigned.

2. Seniority is decided between the employees at the site where the employees are working as per the practice followed before signing of Promotion Policy Settlement.

In consideration of the above, it was decided to promote A. J. Solanki after he completed 2 years of service in Grade M-09.

A grievance was filed by C. M. Sundaram, Stenographer Grade (M-09), Ahmedabad Regional Office, making his claim for the promotion to the position on the following basis.

As per Sl. No. 10, Sub Clause 4 of the Promotion Policy (last para of the sub clause) which is quoted below –

"Normally, for promotion to c particular grade, all the candidates in the grade immediately below that grade would be scrutinised as per the marks system given above. If no suitable candidate is available or if employee refuses promotion then the same process would be followed for each grade below".

The employee further said that he is the senior most employee in the grade directly below the grade for which the vacancy exists in the region as he joined the company on 1st August, 1983 in Grade M-09.

Questions

1. Is Sundaram justified in raising a grievance for promotion?

2. If not Sundaram, who should be promoted as senior clerk at Koyali? Give reasons.

***

Case 6: Demotion – A Tricky Problem

A workman, who committed a grave wrongdoing, was issued a chargesheet which was followed by a domestic enquiry. In the enquiry, the charges were verified. Considering the gravity of the misconduct and past record of service, the management had decided to sack the workman from service. In view of that, he was served the dismissal order, but as there was a conciliation issue pending before the Assistant Commissioner of Labour (Central), though not associated with the dismissal matter, the management had to file an application for approval of its action under Section 33 (2) (b) of the I. D. Act. As a result, the management had passed the dismissal order, but, the workmen went on complete strike for reasons not linked with the dismissal case. The matter went for conciliation before the Assistant Commissioner of Labour (Central), Delhi. Meanwhile, the union president put pressure on the chairman of the firm to revoke the punishment of dismissal to the workman on humanitarian grounds. The workman who was discharged was a significant functionary of the union. Before the CCI

9 (Central), Delhi, an agreement was reached to resolve the on-going strike and one of the clauses was that the management had agreed to revoke the dismissal and demote the workman for three years and transfer him to a distant place. Incidentally, demotion was not included in the list of punishments in this establishment. The workman who was in W-IV grade with ₹ 944 basic was demoted to W-III grade and transferred to a distant place. Replicas of the office order among related parts of the settlement were sent to the payroll department for implementation. Since demotion was unheard of previously in that organisation, many doubts were raised. Ultimately, the payroll department framed the following questions and sought clarification from the personnel department.

Questions

1. In demotion, should the present basic salary be protected?
2. If the present basic salary is beyond the maximum of the lower scale (demoted grade), how should it be treated?
3. Will the workman be entitled to annual increment in the demoted grade?
4. Is the workman entitled to cross the efficiency bar in the operating scale of pay (demoted grade), if he reaches that stage while serving demotion?
5. Is the demotion cumulative or not?
6. After serving the 3-year demotion, where will the workman be fitted in the original grade?
7. What will happen to his seniority, while he is in the demoted grade?
8. If the workman gets a promotional opportunity, while he is in the demoted grade, is he entitled to promotion? If not, how is it treated?
9. What will happen to the seniority or the workman in his original (higher) grade? If he gets a promotional opportunity while serving the demotion, will the workman be entitled to his promotion after his original grade is restored?

***

Case 7: Unwanted Promotion

Kartar Singh joined Lakshmi Bank, Meerut branch as a clerk after getting a post graduate degree in chemistry from Delhi University in 1986. He did his work attentively and was usually rated as a hard-working, ambitious young man. He got the professional qualification, CAIIB, in 1992. After that, he applied for the officers' post under the promotion quota. He did not get the promotion as his scores in the written test were little. For the meantime, he was relocated to Delhi University, campus branch, Delhi. His efforts to scale the career ladder were not successful and after many trials, he intentionally decided to join the ranks of the union as an active member. He became the president of the local branch of Bank Employees' Union in 1995. Because of his interpersonal skills, he moved closer to most employees in the bank and was capable of extinguishing the fires between people rapidly. Lately, he is thought to be a tough union activist to negotiate with and management has developed a kind of negative attitude towards his career moves. In 1996 when the chance came, he was not considered for promotion as his interview scores, this time were not good. The branch manager's confidential report about his union activities is reported to be the major obstruction to his promotion; in the meantime, Kartar Singh started a business of dealership in automobiles using a dummy name. He succeeded significantly in switching the deposits of nearby business community to other banks. On the basis of the suggestions of the new branch manager, management decided to promote Kartar Singh to the officer team in 1999. Recently, Kartar received the appointment order for the officer's post from the head office. The co-workers, along with the branch manager planned an evening tea party, congratulating him for his success. To their surprise, Kartar conveyed his reluctance to accept the offer and immediately declined the promotion, citing medical reasons.

Questions

1. Comment on the promotion policy of the bank, using inputs from the above case.
2. Do you think the management's action of selecting Kartar as an officer after 13 years' of service is in the right direction? Why? Why not?
3. Why did Kartar refuse promotion?

✱✱✱

Case 8: A Case of Transfer at Phillips India

March 16, 1999, was the day that shocked the management of Philips India Limited (PIL). A judgment of the Kolkata High Court restrained the firm from employing the resolution it had passed in the Extraordinary General Meeting (EGM) held in December, 1998. The resolution was to ask for the shareholders' permission to sell the colour television (CTV) factory to Kitchen Appliances Limited, a subsidiary of Videocor.

The judgement came after a long-drawn, bitter battle between the firm and its two unions, namely, Philips Employees Union (PEU) and the Pieco Workers' Union (PWU) over the factory's sale. PEU president Kiron Mehta said, "The company's top management should now see reason. Ours is a good factory and the sale price agreed upon should be reasonable. Further, how come some other firm is ready to take over and hopes to run the firm gainfully when our own management has thrown its hands up, lost hope after investing ₹ 70 crores on the plant".

Philips sources however, refused to accept defeat. The firm instantly disclosed its plans to take further legal action and complete the sale at any cost.

PIL's operation dates back to 1930, when Philips Electricals Co. (India) Ltd., a subsidiary of Holland-based Philips NV was set up. After being initially involved only in trading, PIL established manufacturing facilities in many product lines. PIL started lamp manufacturing in 1938 in Kolkata and followed it up by establishing a radio manufacturing factory in 1948. An electronics components unit was established in Loni, near Pune, in 1959. In 1963, its factory in Kalwa, Maharashtra, started producing electronics measuring equipment. The firm later began to manufacture telecommunication equipment in Kolkata.

PIL wanted to focus its audio and video manufacturing bases of products to different geographic regions.

Corresponding to this decision, the firm transferred its audio product line to Pune. Despite the move that caused displacement of 600 workers, there were no signs of conflict mainly because of the unions' involvement in the overall process. By 1996, PIL's expansion plans had fallen way behind the targeted level.

PIL said that the employees were already overpaid and under productive. The employees retaliated by saying that they kept on working despite the irregular hike in wages.

These differences caused a twenty-month long battle over the wage hike issue; the go-slow tactics of the employees and the failing production brought about huge losses for the firm.

In May 1998, PIL declared its decision to stop operations at Salt Lake and the production was stopped in June 1998. At that time, PWU members agreed to the ₹ 1,178 wage hike offered by the management. This was a retreat from its previous stand when the union, along with the PEU demanded a hike of ₹ 2,000 per employee and other fringe benefits. PEU, on the other hand, refused to move from its position and declined the offer. After a series of negotiations, the unions and the management came to a reasonable agreement on the issue of the wage structure.

Director Ramachandran said that the firm was planning to outsource instead of having its own manufacturing base in the future. The firm selected Pune as its manufacturing base and decided to get the Salt Lake factory off its hands.

In line with this decision, the employees were evaluated and severance packages were announced. Out of 750 employees in the Salt Lake division, 391 employees opted for VRS. Videocon was one of the firms that were approached. PIL decreased the workforce and modernised the unit, spending ₹ 7.1 crores in the process. In September 1998, Videocon agreed to purchase the factory through its nominee, Kitchen Appliances India Ltd. The total worth of the plant was determined to be ₹ 28 crores and Videocon agreed to pay ₹ 9 crores besides taking up the legal responsibility of ₹ 21 crores. Videocon agreed to take over the plant together with the employees as a going concern along with the responsibilities of VRS, provident fund etc.

The PIL Board of Directors met for their decision through a special resolution. After a lot of discussions and clarifications, they finally voted for the resolution. The employees were shocked and, therefore, were angry at the decision. S. N. Roy Choudhary of the Independent Employees Federation in Kolkata said, "The sale will not benefit the firm in any way. As a manufacturing unit, the CTV factory is completely modern with sufficient capacity. It is near to Kolkata port, making shipping of components from far Eastern countries simpler. It constantly gets ISO 9000 certification and has skilled labour. In addition, PIL's major market is in the eastern region".

The unions challenged PIL's plan of selling the CTV unit at such a small price of ₹ 9 crores as in opposition to a valuation of ₹ 30 crores made by the independent valuer, M/s Dalal Consultants. PIL officials said that the sale price was reached after taking into consideration the responsibilities that Videocon would have along with the 360 employees of the plant. This included the gratuity and leave encashment responsibilities of employees who would be included under the same service agreements. The management contended that a VRS offer at the CTV unit would have cost the firm ₹ 21 crores. Denying this, senior members of the union said, "There is no way that a VRS at the CTV unit can set Philips by more than ₹ 9.2 crores".

They explained that PIL officials, by their own admission, have said that around 200 of the 360 employees at the CTV unit are less than 40 years of age and the same number have less than 10 years of work experience.

The unions also said that they wrote to the FIs' about their objection. The employees then approached the Dhoots of Videocon requesting them to pull out from the deal as they were ready to have Videocon as their employer.

Videocon, on the other hand, refused to change its decision. The employees then, filed a petition in the Kolkata High Court challenging PIL's decision to sell the factory to Videocon. The unions approached the firm with an offer of ₹ 10 crores in an attempt to outbid Videocon.

They claimed that they could pay the amount from their provident funds, cooperative savings and personal savings. But PIL declined this offer saying that it was legally bound to sell to Videocon and if the offer fell through, then, the union's offer would be considered together with other interested parties. PIL said that it would not let the employees use the Philips brand and that the employees could not sell the CTVs without it. Furthermore, the employees were taking a great risk by investing their hard-earned savings to take over the plant. Countering this, the employees said that they did not trust Videocon to be a good employer and that it might not be capable of paying their wages. They followed it up with evidences of Videocon's failure to make payments eventually during the course of its business with Philips.

In the last week of December, 1998, employees of PIL spoke to many domestic and multinational CTV makers for a joint venture to run the Salt Lake unit. Kiron Mehta said, "We can always enter into an agreement with a third party. It can be a partnership firm or a joint venture. All alternatives are open. We have already started discussions with several domestic and multinational TV producers." It was added that the union had also spoken to many former PIL directors and employees who they felt could run the plant and were ready to lend a helping hand. Elucidating the point that the employees did not mean to buy out the plant, Mehta said, "If Philips India wants to run the unit again, and then we will surely withdraw the proposal. Do not think that we are intending to take over the plant."

In March, 1999, the Kolkata High Court passed an order restraining any additional deals on the sale of the factory. Justice S. K. Sinha held that the transfer price was too small and PIL had to see it from a more practical point of view.

The insistent PIL filed a petition in the Division bench challenging the trial court's decision. The firm additionally said that the matter was further than the trial court's jurisdiction and its intervention was unnecessary, as the price had been a negotiated one.

The Division bench, on the other hand, did not pass any interim order and PIL moved to the Supreme Court. PIL and Videocon decided to extend their agreement by six months to accommodate the court orders and the employee's confrontation.

In December, 2000, the Supreme Court ultimately passed judgement on the controversial Philips case. It was on the side of the PIL. The judgement dismissed the review petition filed by the employees as a last ditch effort. The judge said that though the employees can demand for their rights, they had no say in any of the policy decisions of the firm, if their interests were not badly affected. After the transfer of ownership, the employment of all employees of the factory was seized by Kitchen Appliances with immediate effect. Consequently, the services of the employees were to be treated as constant and not disrupted by the transfer of ownership. The terms and conditions of employment too were not altered.

Kitchen Appliances began to operate from March 2001. This factory had been selected by Videocon as a main centre to meet the needs of the eastern region market and export to East Asia countries. The Supreme Court decision appeared to be a usual case of 'all's well that ends well' Ashok Nambissan, General Counsel, PIL, said, "The decision taken by the Supreme Court restates the position which Philips has maintained all along that the transaction will be to the benefit of Philips' shareholders." How far the Salt Lake employees agreed with this would perhaps remain unanswered.

Questions

1. Read the case and identify the important points related to HR.

2. What efforts were taken by PIL union for restraining the transfer of the PIL factory to Videocon?

***

2.9 Labour Welfare

Case 1: Employee Welfare Facilities – Organisation's Gain or Strain?

Employee Welfare Facilities – Organisation's Gain or Strain?

United Alliances Limited is a chief cement producer in the country with its subsidiaries based in different areas of the country. The existing products of this firm are 43 and 53 grade cements, bulk cement and ready mix concrete. It has a yearly turnover of ₹ 65 billion and benefits from a major market share in the industry. This firm has a different workforce numbering about 7,500 employees and is recognised for its discipline.

The HR department of United Alliances Limited is managed by Suresh Kumar, who is famous for his insight and perceptiveness. The firm strongly believes in identifying and motivating efficiency. Its compensation policy is mainly based on a performance. As a result, it accords less significance to fixed compensations, be it a direct compensation like basic salary or an indirect one like in employee welfare schemes.

Of late, the management of United Alliances Limited has formulated an ambitious diversification plan to go into the fields of chemical, metal and machine tool production. As the chemical industry is poised for a sharp growth within ten years, United Alliances decided to focus first on the chemical industry in its diversification bid. As a start, it has taken over Vijay Chemicals, one of the leading chemical units in the country. Vijay Chemicals is involved in the production of different chemicals like coal tar, creosote, pitch, anthracene, naphthalene and coat enamel. It has a workforce of 3,200 employees and modern tar distillation plants in three areas. The compensation plan of this firm is different from that of United Alliances Ltd. While United Alliances Ltd. concentrates more on performance-linked pay, the compensation package of Vijay Chemicals has a set compensation with things such as basic salary and welfare schemes as its main constituent. In truth, the latter has been very moderate in employee welfare schemes. This is because the founders of this firm strongly believed that its employees should not worry while doing their work. In accordance with them, provision of sufficient welfare facilities is an important requirement for attaining the required level of employee efficiency, quality and loyalty. The significant welfare facilities of this firm are transport, education, recreation and insurance facilities.

On the other hand, the management of United Alliances Ltd. sees the employee welfare facilities of Vijay Chemicals in a different way and considers it to be a huge financial burden. It also sees it as a stumbling block to the process of attaining cost efficiency in production. It desires tc modernise the compensation package of Vijay Chemicals so as to make it similar to its own compensation package. On the other hand, its HR manager, Suresh Kumar fluctuates with the argument of his management and has advised to the management to continue with the compensation pclicy of Vijay Chemicals. He has long understood that welfare facilities only can create long-term commitment and involvement among the employees. Actually, he has gone a step further and suggested Vijay Chemicals compensation model for his firm. On the other hand, the management of United Allances Ltd. is not convinced by its HR manager's propositions.

Questions

1. What is your opinion of the compensation and welfare packages cf both United Alliances Ltd. and Vijay Chemicals?

2. How do you look at Suresh Kumar's suggestion and the response of his management?

3. If you were to be the HR manager of United Alliances Ltd., what would be your suggestions?

Case 2: Protection of the Rights of the Jethwai's Mine Workers
Protection of the Rights of Jethwai's Mine Workers

The State of Rajasthan has several types of metallic and non-metallic minerals. The workforce employed in the State's mining industry is second only to agriculture. The employees in mining mainly comprise of *adivasis* (tribals) and *dalits* (low castes). These seasonal mine employees engage in hard labour for 12 to 13 hours a day. They work in dangerous conditions, with temperature as high as 50°C in summers and freezing cold in winters. They are prone to numerous occupational diseases and physical irjuries because of the poor safety conditions; the mines do not have basic facilities and do not give even constitutional benefits to the employees. The employers, that is, the mine cwners, are not bothered about the troubles of the employees, as their main motive is to earn proft.

There is a blatant violation of laws and safety measures in most of the mining activities of the state. For instance, certain mining firms work on unlawful or expired leases; they practice inappropriate removal of mine debris; and pay less than the minimum wage to mine workers. Mine owners try to increase profitability by paying miners less for working for long hours and often fail to pay cess or royalties. Small huts are given to miners as shelters that can hardly accommodate them or shield them from weather. It is a tough task for the State Mining Department to control the situation most likely due to lack of political will and the actual resources to completely observe and control the operations of thousands of leases spread across Rajasthan. This disregard has further irritated the already oppressive working conditions of several people. Majority of mine workers are males. Women are mostly involved in activities like clearing debris and pebbles from the mines. They are generally paid far less than male workers, violating all the norms of child labour.

(Prohibition and Regulation) Act, 1986, children are involved in work under dangerous conditions and are exploited in every way.

Jethwai, a small village in the Jaisalmer district of western Rajasthan, is mostly a Bhil tribal village. Aside from Bhils, there are several migrant workers from the neighbouring districts of Jodhpur, Barmen and Ajmer. A large bulk of Jethwai's population is involved in one type of mining-related activity or the other. Migrant population is preferred by mine owners as they are frequently more obedient, and hardly ever complain about unjust treatment or violation of their rights as they fear losing their job. As they are worried about earning their living, such migrant workers agree to work for much lower wages and hardly ever take part in village-based activities.

Generally, the mining industry only reserves some 4 to 5 percent of total production costs for labour. The mine proprietors pay wages in two different ways – daily-wages and piece-rate wages. Even though the mine operators guarantee wages to their labourers at the end of every month, generally such wages are not paid frequently, and workers have to wait for many months to get their wages. To support their families and in situations like marriages, illness or funerals, these mine workers have to borrow huge amount of money from mine owners. Not capable of reimbursing the loan, they are frequently pushed into debt bondage, when they are compelled to work off their debts. For this reason they are given lower wages. This circumstance comes up as these workers do not have any other source of financial support. If they change jobs they need to pay back the complete debt or, time and again, the new employer pays back the debt and the loan is transferred.

Safety conditions in the minefields are not suitable. Accidents often occur in mines because of the primitive manual tools like heavy hammers, chisels, etc. used by the workers. Frequent accidents cause high rate of injuries and numerous deaths every year. Even in this circumstance the mine workers have no help and are forced to borrow from mine owners, and thus fall into the debt trap. Family members of deceased workers get very little compensation; for the most part they are left to fend for themselves.

Disappointed with the Government's lack of concern and the attitude of mine owners a group of environmentalists, lawyers and activists united to form the Mine Labour Protection Campaign (MLPC) in 1994, with the goal of improving the lives and working conditions of Rajasthan's mine workers. The MLPC started its work with the fortitude to defend the rights of mine workers, promote environmental justice, provide adequate healthcare, guarantee occupational safety and warranty fair wages. After staying inactive for a while, the Campaign became active again in 1999 with the creation of a series of mine workers' unions in Rajasthan. In 2001, the Stone Mineworkers' Union (Pathar Khan Mazdoor Union) was created with a total of 95 members. The purpose was to protect the miners' rights and guarantee them safe working conditions. The union worked to guarantee that mine workers received payments on time, and were given safe working conditions, adequate housing, regular employment, and a legally binding guarantee for full compensation in the case of lethal and non-lethal accidents.

The Mine Labour Protection Campaign motivated Jethwai's mine workers to take possession of mining resources by forming a co-operative. This was viewed as an attempt to give mine workers a sense of dignity and a stake in their own land. Their co-operative, the Pathar Khan Shramik Theka Sahkari Samiti Ltd. (PKSTSSL) was created in 2002. Its objective was to help the mine workers take up mining leases, and is one of India's first mining co-operatives for the local people. The PKSTSSL involves in profit-earning activities from mining activities. One of the essential principles of the co-operative is that any profit earned must be circulated equally among all the co-operative members. The wages of workers have increased considerably in comparison to that paid by private mine owners. The co-operative has been earning substantial profits from the time when acquiring of leases to extract minerals became a success, though private mine owners create problems for them. The PKSTSSL educates workers on their legal rights connected to fair wages, working hours and other benefits. Mine workers of co-operative-owned mines have facilities like clean drinking water and suitable shelter rooms.

Motivated by this co-operative, the women of the village have created their own Self Help Group (SHG) that assists its members in developing skills for making products like candles, detergents, etc. and then selling them through SHG shops, thus becoming self-sufficient and supporting their families.

Questions

1. Discuss the problems faced by the mine workers of Rajasthan, as reflected in the case.

2. Which labour laws do you think are contravened in this case?

3. According to you how effective has the MLPC been in mitigating the problems of the mine workers?

4. Discuss the role played by the PKSTSSL in improving welfare of the mine workers. What lessons can mine owners of Rajasthan learn from this co-operative?

Case 3: A Case on Medical Issues in Hindustan Foundry

Hindustan Foundries Ltd., a leading foundry in India, is located in Kolhapur, Maharashtra. The firm supplied castings to all the leading automobile manufacturing firms. In the field of aluminium casting and iron casting techniques, the firm had competent and experienced manpower. The workmen were trained and highly accomplished, and their education level was quite good as compared to other foundries in the state. The firm had 900 permanent employees and, additionally, it employed about 600 employees on contract basis. The firm maintained good industrial relations through wage settlement every four years through collective bargaining.

The firm executed all the terms and conditions agreed in the wage agreement. In the recent wage agreement, the union executed different welfare schemes like subsidised canteens, transport and health care through negotiations.

The firm had a health care tie-up with a very big and well-equipped hospital in Kolhapur. The hospital was managed efficiently and had good facilities in health care. Under the association, the hospital provided services to both out-patients and those patients admitted in the hospital. This facility was available to Hindustan Foundry's employees at an annual premium of ₹ 12,000 p.a. per employee. Every year, the firm paid the premium in lump sum for all the employees. The welfare manager also visited the hospital and took feedback about the services provided to their employees. There were no complaints from the employees about the services provided by the hospital. On the other hand, the union often complained about the services rendered by the said hospital.

Niraj Kumar was the welfare officer working with Hindustan Foundries. He reported to Kunal Singh, the senior manager of human resource. One day while he was completing his daily activities, in his office, he got a call from his boss Kunal Singh. "Niraj, there's been an accident in the factory's moulding shop; would you come over to my cabin immediately."

Niraj rushed to the personnel department. The personnel department was very close to the shop area. On the way, a huge crowd had gathered near the personnel department, the Union members too were present at the site. Most of the employees were just inquisitive spectators, waiting to know exactly what was happening. Niraj managed to reach the injured person whose hands and legs were burnt because of molten metal spatters splashed on his body. The medical officer attending on him was giving him first aid. Kunal Singh called an ambulance immediately, and asked Niraj and the medical officer to move the injured workman to a hospital. He further added that, "We have a tie-up for treatment of the company's employees; please see that the injured workman gets all the required assistance from the hospital."

The crowd led by the union leader formed a fence at the spot and they literally had to shout to move through the crowd. But the union leaders gathered there were not allowing them to carry the workman in the ambulance. The union leaders demanded to take their injured workman to the private hospital instead of the general hospital since the workman had hurt himself while on duty.

The union's demand was backed by a huge crowd gathered at the spot. It was a total siege of the personnel department. The union warned that if the workman is taken to the other hospital, and something happens to him, the whole responsibility would be on the management. Other office-bearers also vouched for poor quality of the tie-up hospital.

Kunal Singh called Niraj to a corner and spoke with him in private. "Niraj, the situation is getting out of hand. We have no choice. Take him to a private hospital, but see that he is not kept there more than three days as the charges there are too high. We should shift him to our hospital as soon as possible."

Niraj rushed the injured employee to a specialised private hospital. Two of the employees came along with him in the ambulance. After reaching the hospital, Niraj showed his visiting card. The injured employee was taken to a specialised ward for treatment. The family of the injured employee was also informed and they also arrived in the hospital. The two co-workers who had come with the injured employee were also happy with the treatment in the hospital and left the hospital after three hours.

Then, Niraj called Kunal Singh and apprised him of the situation. "Niraj, now you need to call up the medical officer of the firm along with the doctor from our tie-up hospital. Take stock of the health of the employee, and see to it that the employee is moved to our tie-up hospital as soon as possible." Niraj replied, "But the union is under the impression that we are continuing the treatment here, sir."

"We will deal with them later. Do as I am telling you. After all, I am answerable to the management; this is an authorised action, so far as I am concerned." Niraj was anxious at the way Kunal was managing the circumstances. But he decided to follow the orders. After all, Kunal Singh was answerable to both the union and the management. The medical officer and the doctor from the tie-up hospital visited and examined the patient, and also had a look-in at the reports and the medicines given to him. The doctors said that at this stage, the patient concerned could be moved to the hospital without difficulty. They guaranteed that the hospital would make a special arrangement to move the patient to their hospital. Niraj left the hospital in the evening and called Kunal and informed him that the injured employee was going to be shifted late in the night. The doctor from the firm's hospital came with the ambulance and moved the patient to their hospital.

The next day, when Niraj reported for duty in the firm, there was a big crowd in front of the personnel department. A group of union representatives were creating a scene. They were upset that the injured employee had been moved out of the specialised private hospital.

Kunal Singh was trying to appease them. He said that "Look, we had committed to you that we would take him to the specialised hospital and we took him there, did we not? Two of his colleagues were witnesses to the admission and the treatment given to him. Now, his condition has improved, so we have taken him to our hospital, where further treatment would be given."

The union members were not happy with what had occurred. The union decided to protest against this incident, as they were not informed before shifting the injured workman. They also decided to hold a general body meeting to reconsider the medical scheme.

Questions

1. What is the main issue in this case?

2. If you were in the place of Kunal Singh, what instructions would you have given to Niraj based on the information given in the case?

3. Are you convinced with the actions taken by the welfare officer, Niraj? What other options would you suggest to Niraj?

4. Comment on the medical scheme provided in Hindustan Foundry.

✳✳✳

2.10 Retrenchment-Layoffs

Case 1: Astrigo Holdings

Astrigo Holdings has a team of 12,000 people whose highest objective is to 'Take Care of Our Customer.' Astrigo Holdings achieves this by selling the highest-quality products at the best price, with the best customer service, world-wide. Great customer service starts with gifted, inventive team members.

The Challenge: Astrigo Holdings had missed its income approximation by 20 cents a share. Profits have fallen down by double digits, irrespective of the hard work put to slash inventory and costs. In spite of aggressive promotions and price cuts, the Astrigo home-improvement stores were losing sales to cheaper retailers who did not even provide good customer service. The recession was hitting the company hard. Even if the firm had millions in the bank due to values passed on by "Pop," Robin (the CEO) didn't want to risk Astrigo's future health by burning that cash now. The firm has a policy of holding a big cash reserve for acquisitions but isn't it a little tough to validate a big bank account simultaneously when people are losing jobs?

An aggressive decrease in head count looked like the only option. "Pop" Astrigo had been compelled to let people go in past recessions but had hated taking such an action. A big layoff would be devastating for the families of the affected employees and for all the towns where Astrigo stores had for a long time been a central fixture.

Robin had asked his executive committee to create teams of two to deal with possible layoff situations, which would then be presented to the Chairman of the Board. This is what they came up with.

Option 1: First In, First Out: A 10 percent decrease in employees would generate sufficient savings to keep profits along the lines of Wall Street's expectations. Robin does not want to reduce more on store acquaintances, because that has an effect on customer service, so the cuts will happen at middle management level with a first in, first out policy. The disadvantages voiced are charges of age discrimination.

Option 2: Performance-Based or Rank-and-Yank: A performance-based layoff based on the next evaluation cycle so as to remove the lowest 10 percent. The firm develops a higher-performing staff. The disadvantages are that people become competitive and are afraid all the time, office politics takes a cruel turn, and the ranking system also needs a lot of effort.

Option 3: Last In, First Out: To look at layoffs as a planned cost-cutting measure is short-sighted. Not only are good people jobless, but layoffs shout to our customers, 'Look at us. We're in trouble.' They hurt individuals' spirits, and that hurts customer service and, in the end, the investors. The problem can best be solved by looking at our overall strategy. The firm exceeded its limits. It could save the money by selling or closing the latest acquisition, Prugh Furniture. It's time to refocus on the core business. Disadvantages are that a great deal of thought and time and hard work go into acquisitions and they're not made carelessly. Eliminating any strategic business units may not be a clever move.

Option 5: Pay Cut: How about taking steps that would let the firm be truthful to its core values? It's necessary to get a bit more creative. Just pick a number. How about a 5 percent across-the-board pay cut, maybe a bigger one for people making six figures? Astrigo is not a union shop and so has the flexibility to do it. Disadvantages are the pushback but isn't that better than the alternatives?

Solution

STEP 1: Re-examine strategic goals: Concentrate on your core business or concentrate on your most profitable business. Consolidate, lose a unit, or go back to the basics. Prioritise and re-assess spending, but do it selectively. Boost the revenue-generating budgets that have a high ROI (Return on Investment) and completely discontinue the support budgets that have not delivered value. Put a stop to any widespread reorganisation or transitions. Re-examine your firm's history, and put yourself in the founder's shoes, what would you need to do to stay alive? Ask why the firm is doing what it is doing. If it makes sense keep it, if it does not, lose it.

STEP 2: Look at adversity as an opportunity: Sack those employees who are not performing well and who have slipped through the cracks through performance-based job cuts.

STEP 3: Involve the entire team: People are concerned, emotional infectivity has overtaken all motivation, negative energy in the air has killed an employee's focus and productivity, and the overwhelming stress of layoffs is creating a spike in illness. Skip all this nonsense by making the issue clear all through the firm. Let people understand that they are still there and that is on purpose and they are very much required to either step it up or step on out. Instruct managers to redefine their department's goals to be similar to the firm's new shift in strategy and redistribute work to be most effective and concentrate the energy on what is most required. The worst case scenario is pay cuts across the board. Keep all but the most excessive profits.

Questions

1. Analyse the options that are stated here in detail.
2. Examine the solutions and accordingly recommend better solutions.

Case 2: A Case on Pratibha Plastics

Pratibha Plastics is a 10-year-old firm that is based in Aurangabad, the firm employs 250 workmen. The firm is into manufacturing plastic moulding parts that are used in automobile, air conditioning, etc.

The firm had an internal union, but has had its share of conflicts on many occasions for the last two years. After eight months of discussions, they had signed a settlement on December, 2007. One of the clauses to the said settlement was – If the firm could not continue its production because of reasons beyond the control of management, then, it could declare a layoff and employees would then get 50 percent of their basic salary +dearness allowance.

In May 2008 when there was global recession, the sale of automobile air conditioners was hit badly. This caused a decrease in the demand for their product. As the inventory was building up, the management decided to declare a 'layoff' for four weeks, starting from 15th May, 2008. The said decision was also conveyed to the union.

As the time of 'layoff' was to be for a month, it meant many of the workmen would be receiving less than half of their wages. Thus, they informed the union president about their concern. The union requested the management to reconsider the decision and requested the management to decrease the 'layoff' period in case it was not in a position to give an advance as 'interim payment.' On the other hand, the management refused this request stating they could not pay as they were facing acute shortage of working capital (cash flow).

Questions

1. As an HR manager, what decision would you take on the above situation and why?

2. What proactive actions would you like to suggest for handling such situations in future?

Case 3: A Case on Layoff and Dispute

Forty-two years ago, One of India's leading business houses, chose to establish their plant near Pune. The group was well-known for its ethics in business, community development activities and was the pioneer in introducing different labour welfare schemes. Post independence, these welfare schemes became model laws when the Government of India chose to pass the Factory Act, 1948.

The said factory had 10,000 workers and 2,000 staff members. All the workers in the factory were members of union. All agreements that were signed between the management and the union were for a period of three years. The employees of the factory were amongst the better paid in the region/industry with regards to money and welfare facilities. The main product of the firm included designing and manufacturing of commercial vehicles and machine tools.

Over the last thirty years, the factory had enjoyed pleasant industrial relations. On the other hand, during the late 90s, the firm faced a serious labour problem. The firm had internal unions which did not have any affiliation with any external political or other trade union. The last such major incident was reported way back in 1987. This happened in response to the management's introducing 'work cells' in one of the production units, where the operator was needed to work on 2-3 machines at the same time. The union opposed this, and, resorted to 'tool down' agitation, which was conducted in the whole unit lasting six days. After thoroughly explaining the concept to all those concerned and with the additional benefit of multi machines, the problem was resolved to the satisfaction of the union. Otherwise, generally, the relations between the union and the management were always pleasant.

In 1992, one more incident took place. The firm's overall performance was not good, and so for the first time they offered a bonus at a lesser rate, that is, almost by ₹ 500, than the previous corresponding year. In the beginning, the union was not ready to accept the bonus, but as the festival of Diwali was approaching, the union on the face of increasing pressure was exposed as a divided house over this issue, with some even opting to sign for the bonus.

On the other hand, at this point, an unrecognised external union managed to successfully make inroads into the firm by riding on the discontentment of some of the employees who were not happy with the decision of the recognised union. During an incident of violence in the firm between these two union members, one of the managing committee members was issued a chargesheet, and suspended with an enquiry pending against him. During that time, the settlement discussions had started. Surprisingly, because of pressure from the external union supporters, the suspended union managing committee member, Krishnan was selected as a member of the negotiation committee.

The management did not approve Krishnan's name on the negotiation committee of the union. They were not ready to go ahead with negotiations with Krishnan on the negotiation committee. This disturbed the relations between the union and management and some more bad cases of stoppage of work were reported. The workmen in the premises were also called to meetings where they were provoked, and incidents of abusing the supervisors also started happening on a regular basis. In a couple of weeks, the protests spread on a big scale across the organisation. There was a mass boycott over breakfast and lunch, also practiced by some union members and which was supported by external union.

On a particular Friday, the shift 'A' workers coming in at 6.15 a.m. was beaten *en masse* at the entry gate of the plant. About seventy supervisors and workmen were targeted and were roughly beaten by company employees and the members of the unrecognised external union. Some of them had to be hospitalised. This incident brought the firm's work to a grinding halt.

The firm took this incident very seriously and suspended about thirty-six workmen by issuing those charge sheets. The incident affected the industrial relations in the firm badly. After the management action, all the workmen went on strike with the following demands –

(a) Withdrawing all the thirty-six suspension orders and reinstating all of them.

(b) Meetings on negotiations with Krishnan on the committee.

(c) The management, nevertheless, rejected these demands. The strike began, and continued for a long time. As the institution was a big one, other industries too felt the effect of this strike. To publicise the strike and to get the backing of others, some of the workmen proposed to protest in Pune, a central location, so that they could get public sympathy. Thus, the union decided to gather at Shaniwar Wada. About 5,000 workers gathered at Shaniwar Wada for staging a strike against the management.

(d) The issue was raised at the State Assembly too. One of the ministers in the local area intervened in this issue. He called both the union representatives and management representatives and tried to find a solution, but as the union was in no mood to listen, they could not find a reasonable solution to end the strike. After a month, the Chief Minister ordered the protestors to leave the place. With help of the police, all the workmen were moved to jail on charges of violence and disturbance at a public place.

Questions

1. What are the main issues in the above case? Highlight the main points in this case.

2. What suggestions would you give to the management? What proactive actions would you like to suggest?

3. Do you justify the actions taken by the union?

Case 4: Between a Rock and a Hard Place – A Case on Downsizing

The department of Human Resources manages Workers' Compensation Insurance, Unemployment Insurance, and various employment and training programs. We do it with 150 less employees than we did 16 months ago. Real dollar cutbacks in federal funding have ruthlessly cut into our capability to support our operations. Unlike most other cabinet-level agencies, the department of Human Resources is 99 percent funded by federal fees. Like most state agencies, personnel salaries and benefits are more than 80 percent of our total cost. When the federal budget takes a bite out of our budget, the only recourse is to decrease staffing. That is a polite substitute for firing real people. It's a difficult thing to do.

In January 1995, the department had 1,079 full-time positions and about 1,000 people on the payroll. The new administration inherited a funding problem that had been building for five years. Shifting personnel and costs between programs and funds had prohibited layoffs during that time. The bill came payable with the change of administration. Unemployment insurance funds decreased about 10 percent this year. Employment and training funds took a greater hit. Altogether, the department received about 56 million less this year than last year. That was a 15 percent reduction. Again, I point out that this was a real dollar decrease, not a usual inside-the-be tway decrease in the increase.

Our programs are on staggered fiscal years, so the budget reality came home in July and then was supported with additional funding cuts in October. In July, we established a hiring freeze to take the benefits of attrition. About fifty people left the payroll and were not substituted. By October, it was clear that a layoff would happen, and we spent the next three months going through all the hoops and barrels at the divisions of personnel services in the department of administration. This was a learning experience for us as well. The most senior employee there could not remember when the state last had a layoff." We were rewriting the book. The "bureaucracy myth" is not always fair, but in this case, it took us until the day of the scheduled layoff before all the process was accepted and paperwork cleared. We struggled with hold-ups, delays and paper shuffling to no end. Every time we thought we were good-to-go, another person had to bless everything".

We were communicating continuously with employees, talking about budgets, revenues, costs. Layoffs were talked about for a long time. Positions for abolishment were recognised on the basis of the requirement to get the job done. All local offices were run though a staffing formula and nine were recognised as too small to function at the forthcoming reduced staffing levels. These offices were declared for closing the same day as the layoff letters were mailed and layoff announcements made.

In spite of our efforts to be open and clear, many employees were shocked and in doubt that layoffs actually happened and that offices were actually locked. The culture of governmental/bureaucratic invincibility that has developed over the last three decades made it impossible for the employees to believe what they were being told. The theory of government growth shifted, and they were blinded by their old ways of thinking about government employment.

We established contact teams to help laid-off employees with unemployment benefits and job placement. The secretary made special contacts for many employees to gain placement at other state agencies. We wrote many letters of reference. Some laid-off workers were re-employed within our department temporarily because of the unexpected arrival of a special grant. All these efforts helped ease the situation.

On the other hand, after all the bumping rights were used, the layoff had an effect on more than 300 of the 1,000 employees in the department, either through demotion, reduction in pay, or termination. With one third of our department family dysfunctional, performing even daily functions was hard. It took a lot of planning to guarantee that the public still received services throughout this time. It is a credit to all our public employees that little commotion occurred.

Because of civil service regulations and policies, seniority still rules in our state government. Among the saddest chores of management is to inform highly accomplished, fresh, young public employees and administrators that they will be laid-off while older, less effective employees remain. The questions of equity, individual rights, and efficiency cut in many directions.

Now, with government shutdown, block-grant proposals, devolution to the states, and election-year posturing, we are preparing for additional cuts and taking steps to plan for future layoffs. It is naive to take for granted that, though our department and others are downsizing, it is only beginning.

Questions

1. The authors raise a number of concerns about the functioning of the agency. After identifying the problems the author separates them into those which can be addressed (if at all) by (a) elected and appointed officials, (b) managers and supervisors, (c) the personnel director, (d) employees.

2. What are the solutions to those problems that you identified as resolvable in your response to question 1? For each solution, specify the person or group responsible for implementing it, and how you would recommend they work to overcome any implementation barriers.

3. For those problems, that are not resolvable under current conditions, specify the changes that would have to occur for the problem to be solved? How bad would things have to get? How would that make the problem resolvable?

4. If you were a manager in this organisation, how would you deal with employee anxiety and the performance issues it can create?

✱✱✱

2.11 VRS

Case 1: A Case on VRS Problems in State Bank of India

In February 2001, India's largest public sector bank (PSB), namely, the State Bank of India (SBI) faced severe opposition from its employees over a Voluntary Retirement Scheme (VRS). The VRS, which was approved by the SBI board in December, 2000, was in response to Federation of Indian Chambers of Commerce and Industry's (FICCI) report on the banking industry. The report said that the Indian banking industry was overstaffed by as much as 35 percent.

In order to reduce employees and the staff costs, the government declared that it would be decreasing its manpower. Following this, the Indian Banks Association (IBA) formulated a VRS package for the PSBs, which was approved by the Finance Ministry. Though SBI promoted the VRS as a 'Golden Handshake', its employee unions perceived it to be a retrenchment scheme. They said that the VRS was unnecessary, and that the real problem, which plagued the bank were non-performing assets. The unions argued that the VRS might force to close the rural branches because of acute manpower shortage. This was expected to affect SBI's aim to improve economic conditions by providing necessary financial aid to rural areas.

The unions also alleged that the VRS decision was taken without undertaking an exercise of proper manpower planning. In February 2001, the SBI issued a directive changing the eligibility criteria for VRS for the officers by saying that only those officers who had crossed their fifty-five years of age would be granted VRS. As a result, the applications of around 12,000 officers were declined.

The officers who were denied the chance to opt for the VRS formed an Association – 'SBI VRS Optee Officers' Association to oppose this SBI directive. The association claimed that the management was adopting discriminatory policies in granting the VRS. The average estimated cost per head for execution of VRS for SBI and its seven connected banks worked out to ₹ 0.65 million and ₹ 0.57 million, respectively. As a result of the VRS, SBI's net profit decreased from ₹ 25 billion in 1999-00 to ₹ 16 billion in 2000-01.

The SBI was the biggest bank in India with regards to network of branches, revenues and workforce. It offered an extensive range of services for both personal and corporate banking. The personal banking services included credit cards, housing loans, consumer loans, and insurance. For corporate banking, SBI offered infrastructure finance, cash management and loan syndication. Over the years, the bank became saddled with a big workforce and huge non-performing assets.

According to reports, staff costs in 1999-2000 amounted to ₹ 4.5 billion as against ₹ 4.1 billion in 1998-99. Increased competition from the New Private Sector Banks (NPBs) further added to SBI's problems. The new private sector banks had effectively leveraged technology to compensate for their size. Though SBI had 9,000 branches, a mere 22 percent of those 1935 branches were linked through Internet.

In contrast, all of HDFC Bank's 61 branches were linked. By 2000, SBI's net profit per employee was ₹ 0.43 million; while HDFC's was ` 0.96 million, and SBI's NPA level was around 7.18 percent as against HDFC's 0.73 percent. The analysts remarked that the very factors that were once hailed as the strengths of SBI – reach, customer base and experience – had turned out to be its weaknesses.

Those apart, technological tools like ATMs and the Internet had changed banking dynamics. After the computerisation of banks, a big part of the back office staff had become redundant.

To protect its business and remain profitable, SBI realised that it would have to decrease its cost of operations and increase its revenues from fee-based services. The VRS implementation thus formed a part of an overall cost-cutting initiative.

The VRS package offered sixty days salary for every year of service or the salary to be drawn by the employee for the remaining period of service, whichever was less.

While 50 percent of the payment was to be paid instantly, the rest could be paid in cash or bonds. An employee could avail of the pension or provident fund as per his choice. The package that was mentioned before was offered to the permanent staff that had put in a minimum of fifteen years of service or was 40 years old. as of March 31, 2000.

The SBI was shocked at the unprecedented protest its VRS elicited from their employees. The unions claimed that the move would cause acute shortage of manpower in the bank and that the bank's decision was taken in haste without planning properly. They added that the VRS would not be feasible as there was an acute lack of officers in the rural and semi-urban areas where the branches were not yet computerised.

Furthermore, the unions alleged that the management was compelling its employees to select the VRS route. They said that the threat of bringing down the retirement age from 60 years to 58 years was putting a lot of pressure on senior bank officials to select the scheme. In December 2000, SBI had formed a joint venture with the French insurance company Cardif, a branch of BNP Paribas Assurance, for entering into the life insurance business.

The unions questioned the logic behind expanding the business and reducing the staff strength. They argued that this move would considerably increase the workforce burden and, as a result, adversely affect customer service. In 2000, SBI had undertaken a large-scale clientele membership drive in some states to attract more customers.

The unions opined that the VRS could prove to be counterproductive as the increased business might not be handled correctly. On the other hand, in spite of all the protests, SBI received around 35,000 applications for the VRS. The analysts were quick to indicate that many bank employees opted for the VRS for availing better prospects offered by the NPBs. SBI had not anticipated such a huge response to the scheme. While the VRS was mainly aimed at decreasing the clerical staff and sub-staff, the maximum number of optees turned out to be from the officer cadre. The clerical staff, on the other hand, was reluctant to opt for the VRS, as they feared low employment opportunities for them in the non private bank sectors. According to reports, the number of applications from officers stood at 19,295 which meant that over 33 percent of the total officers in the bank had sought VRS.

Questions

1. What issues were raised by the State Bank union in the VRS?

2. Was the management objective fulfilled by receiving a very good response on VRS? What were the problems that arose after receiving the applications for VRS?

3. Read the case carefully and identify five main points in the above case study with their importance.

✱✱✱

Case 2: VRS Case Study of SAIL

SAIL was formed in 1973 as a holding company of the government- owned steel and connected input firms. In 1978, the subsidiary firms including Durgapur Mishra Ispat Ltd., Bokaro Steels Ltd., Hindustan Steel Works Ltd., Salem Steel Ltd., and SAIL International Ltd., were all dissolved and merged with SAIL. The Durgapur and Bhilai plants were mainly manufacturing long products whereas the Rourkela and Bokaro plants had facilities for manufacturing flat products. SAIL was the world's tenth biggest and India's biggest steel manufacturer with a 33 percent share in the domestic market. In the financial year 1999-2000, the firm generated revenues of ₹ 162.5 billion and incurred a net loss of ₹ 17.2 billion.

In February, 2000, the SAIL management decided a financial and business restructuring plan recommended by McKinsey & Co., a leading global management-consulting company. The McKinsey report proposed that SAIL reorganise into two strategic business units (SBUs) – a flat products company and a long products company.

As intense competition was expected in this area, the plant that was visualised put the flat products company on the block first, and the long products company at a later date. They also suggested decreasing manpower through the Voluntary Retirement Scheme (VRS).

McKinsey also suggested in his business restructuring proposals, the divestment of the following non-core assets –

- Power plants at Rourkela, Durgapur and Bokaro, Oxygen Plant-2 of the Bhilai Steel Plant and the Fertiliser Plant at Rourkela.

- Salem Steel Plant (SSP), Salem.

- Alloy Steel Plant (ASP), Durgapur.

- Visveswaraya Iron and Steel Plant (VISL), Bhadravati.

- Conversion of IISCO into a joint venture with SAIL having only minority shareholding.

The major concern for SAIL was the firm's 1,60,000-strong workforce. Manpower costs alone accounted for 17 percent of the firm's gross sales in 1999-2000. This was the biggest percentage, when compared with other steel producers such as Essar Steel (1.47 percent) and Ispat Industries (1.34 percent).

There was excess manpower in the non-plant departments. Around 30 percent of SAIL's manpower, including executives was in the non-plant departments, just adding to the superfluous paperwork. Hindustan Steel, SAIL's predecessor was modelled on government secretariats, with thousands of clerks and messengers together with a few departmental heads and managers. A senior official remarked: "If you walk into any SAIL office anywhere, you will find people chatting, reading novels, knitting, and so on. Thousands of them just do not have any work. This area has not even been considered as a focus area for the present VRS, possibly because these people were the administrators of the whole plant and no one wants to think of them as surplus."

With 60,000 employees in these offices and non-plant departments like schools, township activities etc, SAIL could well bring these down to less than 10,000. Decrease in white-collar manpower needed a change in the systems of office work and record-keeping, and a very high level of computerisation. Officers across the organisation employed many stenographers and assistants. Signing on note sheets was a status symbol for SAIL officers. Another official commented, "Systems have to be result-oriented rather than person-oriented and responsibilities must match rewards and recognition. There is a need to change the mindset of the management, before specific plans can be drawn out for reduction of office staff."

From the start, SAIL had to deal with political intervention and pressure. It is time that the top management takes a tough stand on such matters. One does not have to call in McKinsey to decide that many SAIL stockyards and branch offices are redundant."

As a part of the restructuring plan, McKinsey had recommended that by the end of 2003, the management of the firm needed to cut the 160,000-strong labour force to 100,000, through VRS. The management was banking on natural attrition to decrease the number by 45,000 within two years, but the government's decision to increase the retirement age to sixty further delayed the reduction. SAIL launched a VRS in mid-1998 for employees who had worked for a minimum period of twenty years or were fifty years in age or above.

The scheme provided an income that was equal to 100 percent of the prevailing basic pay and dearness allowance to the eligible employees. About 5,975 employees chose the scheme. Of them, 5,317 were executives and 658 non-executives. Most of those who opted were above 55 years. On 31st March, 1999, SAIL introduced a 'sabbatical leave scheme', under which the employees could take a break from the firm for two years for studies/employment elsewhere, with the option of rejoining the firm (if they wanted to) at the end of the time. The sabbatical allowed the younger members of the SAIL employees to leave without pay for 'self-renewal, enhancement of expertise/knowledge and experimentation,' which broadly translated into higher studies or even new employment.

On 1st June, 1999, SAIL launched another VRS for its employees. Employees who had completed a minimum of fifteen years of service or were forty years or above could choose the scheme. The new VRS, which was opened to all employees of the firm, was operational till the 31st January, 2000. Its target groups included:

- Those who were habitual absentees, regularly ill and those who were additional due to the closure of plants and mines and
- Poor performers

Under the new package, the employees who chose the scheme, depending on their age, would get a monthly income as a percentage of their existing basic salary and dearness allowance (DA) for the remaining years of their services, till superannuation. However, the employees above the age of fifty-five years were given 105 percent of the basic pay and dearness allowance (DA) every month. Those employees who were between the ages of fifty-two and fifty-five years got 95 percent of the basic pay and dearness allowance; while those below the age of fifty-two years got 85 percent of the basic pay and dearness allowance.

The new scheme, like the old one was a deferred payment scheme, with extra carrots like a 5 percent raise in monthly benefits for each of the three age groups. By September 1999, over 4,000 employees chose the new scheme. About 1,700 employees chose VRS in the Durgapur Steel Plant; while in the Bhilai, Bokaro and Rourkela steel plants, the number differed between 400 and 700. In September 2000, SAIL declared yet another round of VRS, in a bid to remove 10,000 employees by the end of March 2001.

SAIL ended its four-year recruitment freeze by announcing its plans to fill up more than 250 posts at its different plant sites in both technical and non-technical categories.

In mid 1998, in a bid to persuade its employees to accept VRS, SAIL emphasised on six 'plus' points of VRS, in its internal communiqué *Varta*. The points were as follows –

During the next four to five years, SAIL has to decrease its employees by 60,000 for its own continued existence. Employees with chronic ailments, and habitual absentees, who added to low productivity, had to go first – maybe, with the help of administrative actions.

1. The employees may have to be transferred to any other part of the country in the larger interest of the firm.

2. For those who began their career as healthy young men 25-30 years ago, the VRS will take care of their financial worries significantly, and they can discharge their domestic duties more comfortably.

3. VRS can be used for special reasons like paying a lot of money for getting one's son admitted to a professional course.

4. VRS will give many people the money and time on pursuing personal dreams. It is a good chance to do social service.

The trade unions were on a warpath against the suggestions of McKinsey. Posters put up by the Centre of Indian Trade Unions (CITU) at SAIL's central marketing office said that the McKinsey report was meant not for the revival or survival of SAIL, but for its burial. The TU leaders felt that SAIL would try to reinforce support for the financial restructuring proposal based on the suggestions of McKinsey.

But being a government-owned company, SAIL cannot take decisions on such suggestions as the privatisation of SAIL or breaking it up into two product-based firms. Even in comparatively small matters like the hiving off of power plants to a subsidiary firm, with SAIL being the main partner, the government had not cleared SAIL's proposal, even after months of gestation. Thus, it was futile to think that SAIL would get the permission of the government to sell off Salem Steel Plant (SSP) in Tamil Nadu or shut down Alloy Steels Plant (ASP) at Durgapur in West Bengal.

At SSP, all the TUs had joined hands to form a 'Save Salem Steel Committee' and observed a day's token strike on 24th June, 1999, demanding investment in SSP by SAIL rather than by a private partner.

Though TUs had no opposition to voluntary retirements, they were not very happy about the circumstances. They were worried that employment opportunities were reducing in the steel industry and that decrease in manpower would mean increasing the number of contractors and their employees. After the Rourkela Steel Plant in Orissa absorbed the contractors' workers on Supreme Court orders, fresh contractors had been employed to fill up the vacancies. SAIL TU leaders were insistent that the McKinsey suggestions were not the last word or SAIL.

They felt that foreign consultancy companies were not capable of appreciating the role played by major public sector units like SAIL or Indian Oil in the growth of the Indian economy. They suspected that since big public sector units had shown they could endure the onslaught of other multi-national companies; efforts were being made to weaken them, break them into pieces and ultimately privatise them. On February, 17, two thousand employees at SSP went on a strike against the government's decision to restructure SAIL. The strike was called by eight unions affiliated to CITU, INTUC, ADMK and PMK. CITU secretary Tapan Sen said – "The unions are going to serve the ultimatum to the government for indefinite action in the days to come if this retrograde decision is not reversed. Demonstrations will be held against the government's decision in all steel plants and workers of Durgapur would hold a day-long *dharna*. Steel workers all over the country, irrespective of their affiliations reacted sharply to the disastrous and deceptive decision of the government on the so-called restructuring of SAIL."

Questions

1. Identify the main points in the case study.

2. Identify the points that were illustrated in the above case which led to organisational inefficiency in terms of utilisation of manpower.

3. Being a human resource management student, critically examine the VRS offered by the management. Give your suggestions to improve the scheme.

Case 3: Case Study in Restructuring Manpower: VRS in Whirlpool

The parent firm, Whirlpool Corporation, USA, took over management control of the Faridabad based plant, Kelvinator of India in February 1995. As a part of the parent firm's restructuring plan, the first main concern was to underline the need to reduce the strong workforce of 2,500 white collar employees by 40 percent in the newly acquired Indian outfit. The management knew about the legal position prevailing in India on decrease in manpower and therefore, it chose to win over the confidence of the employees and their trade unions for a smooth switch.

To start with, the local management started weekly meetings with the employees. To make the firm more competitive and successful in the market was the meeting's main agenda. In addition to that, the programme included the plant manager's objectives, strategies, the market competitors, and how to excel in the rigid competitive market. The management was capable of making an impression on the employees, the firm's dire need to restructure and so change was an absolute necessity in the way the company operated. The managers of the corporation also visited the plant repeatedly and also addressed the employees on the plant management's plan for restructuring.

The staff started to appreciate the firm's concerns for change. Consequently, the message was communicated that the current ways of working required revaluation and certain number of the employees will have to go out while new job opportunities would be formed; this message went well with the employees. The employees slowly started sharing the concerns of the management and a voluntary retirement scheme was designed.

In the beginning, VRS was started for three months in June 1995. The scheme offered three months wages as severance payment for each year of service left over. A lump sum amount was paid to those who had worked only for four years. The scheme was capable of catching the attention of fifty to sixty percent of the staff. On the basis of skill analysis and potential for retraining/redeployment 1000 staff were given VRS.

The plant management being aware of the growing need to develop and maintain the confidence of the existing staff started a reassurance drive. The management started what was called as 'policy deployment tool' (PDT) which was meant to speak with the employee in general, the gains arising out of VRS, in addition to the firm's long and short-term goals at each opening level. Additionally, it involved a directive on how every employee can contribute to organisational objectives, emphasising the important areas of his job, his expected role in the job in addition to the road map of his career in the firm. In the meantime, the plant management went on to improve the facilities for the staff.

Next, as a follow-up of the PDT, the management introduced what was termed as the Whirlpool Excellence System Module (WES). WES was a control measure on staff performance. WES concentrated on assessment of staff performance taking into consideration the new system. Later, the firm introduced 'people commitment survey' (PCS) for measurement of the level of staff satisfaction from the new measures taken to improve staff facilities.

The firm had developed an effective communication system with the staff to 'tell and sell' their aims and objectives, organisational expectations from each staff member and the career growth designed for everyone. Consequently, it became easy for the management to enlist support in its efforts for excellence. Feedback on good as well as bad performance to the staff was an important built-in process in the communication system and this technique paid dividends to the management.

Questions

1. Analyse the VRS implemented in this company.
2. Identify the main points in the case study.

Case 4: Hindustan Gear Company Ltd.

Hindustan Gear Company Limited, a heavy gear manufacturing firm had been incurring heavy losses for the last three years. Its market share dropped from the earlier 30 percent to 5 percent in the heavy gear sector. The plant head, Rahul Kumar, was not confident of performing any better in the upcoming years, as their previous clients had now started importing the same (gears and other components) from China, as they were 30 percent much cheaper. Rahul Kumar, thus, selected a 'cross functional committee' to study the aforementioned issue and submit a report.

The study brought to light the following major facts –

1. The manufacturing division had 25 percent excess manpower.
2. The productivity of the company was 40 percent lower than a benchmarked company.
3. The above points had a bad effect on the cost of the products, which was 25 percent higher. In other words, their profit margin was also lower by that percentage.
4. With 25 percent excess manpower, the workmen were given 10 percent average overtime, which further added to the costs.

After studying the report, Rahul Kumar called a meeting of all the departmental heads. After holding discussions with them, he decided to decrease costs by decreasing manpower from 850 to 750. He asked the HR head to give the details of the manpower, such as age and other significant observations about their past track record on productivity and of the personal problems connected to productivity like medical problems, absenteeism etc.

The HR head submitted the following report –

Employee Category	Age Group			Other Problems Related To Productivity
	> 50 years	> 45 years	> 30 years	
Workmen	60	20	50	
Supervisors/Staff	10	20	28	
Workmen with medical problems and absentee cases.				20

After holding discussions and getting feedback of the HR head on the above report, Rahul Kumar decided to come up with a VRS scheme that targeted 50 and above age group employees and workmen with medical problems and high absenteeism cases. The aim was to decrease manpower by 100 cases from the aforesaid groups.

The HR head called a meeting of the union, and explained all the details of the VRS scheme to the union members. The union members said that they would agree with the scheme if it was a satisfactory financial package. The HR head then prepared a proposal of the VRS and submitted it to the managing director for his approval. Rahul Kumar checked with the finance head about the financial effect of the package and after discussions with them; he gave his approval to the VRS scheme. The package was as follows –

(a) This VRS scheme given to the employees is subject to management's discretion.

(b) If an employee chooses the Voluntary Retirement Scheme, he would be paid ₹ 1,00,000 in cash and a monthly pension of 50 percent of his Basic + dearness allowance up to the age of retirement, or a ₹ 15,00,000 as lump sum payment.

The union gave their consent to the said scheme. About 107 employees applied for the scheme. On the other hand, out of 107, 17 employees in the age group of 40 to 50 years were good performers. Thus, the management decided not to give VRS to these seventeen employees.

In response to the same, the union objected strongly and told the management that if these seventeen employees were also not given VRS, then, none of the employees would choose VRS. The HR department, ultimately gave in to this union's demand and decided to release all the employees.

Questions

1. Suggest ways to implement the VRS as desired by the management.

2. If you are an HR head at Hindustan Gears Ltd., how would you have handled this situation?

***

Case 5: VRS of Garuda Enterprises

Garuda Enterprises, Ltd. is a public limited firm that employs more than 1600 regular employees apart from about 250 contract employees. There is a strong union operating in the firm and the management-union relations are friendly. January 2011 was the month when several employees were on leave and management had taken action against some employees who did not come to work and had not taken a leave during 2010. Both these were a regular trait in the firm every January.

This January 2011, however, the firm decided to launch a VRS scheme to decrease its permanent workforce and rationalise the manpower. The scheme was worked out and published for the employees on 27th January. The scheme stated that employees must submit their applications on or before 31st January, 2011 and management would decide whether to accept or not to accept the VRS applications.

Among the different applicants there were two applicants against whom action for absence without leave was initiated and one applicant who was on leave during 27 to 31 January. The two applicants against whom action was taken submitted their applications on 28th and 29th January respectively. The third applicant who was on leave, resumed on 4th February 2011 and then submitted his application on 5th February, 2011.

The firm considered all applications and refused some applications including these three applications. The reasons forwarded by the firm were that in case of two employees, disciplinary action was in process and in case of the third employee he had submitted his application after the due date, that is, 31st January 2011. Towards end of February the two employees were awarded punishment of 2 days suspension without wages.

Upon hearing that their applications were rejected, the three employees went to the union and the union was now agitated about the action of management in not accepting the VRS application of these three employees.

Questions

1. Is the action of management right? How?
2. What can the union do in this respect?
3. What should be the principles involved in operating a VRS scheme?

***

www.ingramcontent.com/pod-product-compliance
Lightning Source LLC
Chambersburg PA
CBHW080825020726
47501CB00009B/2425